"A

The grey man

"Are we...guests

Gog smiled, a re   unlike Magog's, and I saw
that he was missing his bottom front teeth.

"Oh, we're not guests, Miss. We definitely broke in."

I squelched my alarm at the alacrity with which he said
that we were committing what had to be felony, even in
Europe.

"How did you find it?" Anyan asked, casually.

"Facebook," Gog said. "You'd be amazed at what people put on their walls. This young couple is enjoying a
weekend in Amsterdam. It was very nice of them to let us
know exact dates, don't you think?"

I shook my head, very glad that for all intents and pur-
poses, I lived in 1996. Having no friends, I'd never been
up on social networking.

And now I had no inclination to start.

Praise for the Jane True series

"Jane is sure to endear herself to new readers with her
charm, sass, and vulnerability, while longtime fans will
be thrilled by her magical and emotional growth."
    —**Publishers Weekly**

"Peeler is like the Janet Evanovich of paranormal
fantasy..."
    —**Paul Goat Allen, bn.com**

By Nicole Peeler

JANE TRUE NOVELS

Tempest Rising
Tracking the Tempest
Tempest's Legacy
Eye of the Tempest
Tempest's Fury

MURDER AND SALUTATIONS

A Card-Making Mystery

Elizabeth Bright

A SIGNET BOOK

SIGNET
Published by New American Library, a division of
Penguin Group (USA) Inc., 375 Hudson Street,
New York, New York 10014, USA
Penguin Group (Canada), 90 Eglinton Avenue East, Suite 700, Toronto,
Ontario M4P 2Y3, Canada (a division of Pearson Penguin Canada Inc.)
Penguin Books Ltd., 80 Strand, London WC2R 0RL, England
Penguin Ireland, 25 St. Stephen's Green, Dublin 2,
Ireland (a division of Penguin Books Ltd.)
Penguin Group (Australia), 250 Camberwell Road, Camberwell, Victoria 3124,
Australia (a division of Pearson Australia Group Pty. Ltd.)
Penguin Books India Pvt. Ltd., 11 Community Centre, Panchsheel Park,
New Delhi - 110 017, India
Penguin Group (NZ), cnr Airborne and Rosedale Roads, Albany,
Auckland 1310, New Zealand (a division of Pearson New Zealand Ltd.)
Penguin Books (South Africa) (Pty.) Ltd., 24 Sturdee Avenue,
Rosebank, Johannesburg 2196, South Africa

Penguin Books Ltd., Registered Offices:
80 Strand, London WC2R 0RL, England

First published by Signet, an imprint of New American Library,
a division of Penguin Group (USA) Inc.

First Printing, December 2006
10 9 8 7 6 5 4 3 2 1

With my deepest admiration and respect,
To my mentor and hero,
Tim Myers

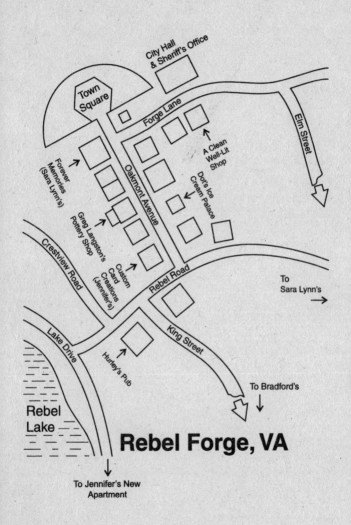

City Hall & Sheriff's Office

Town Square

Forge Lane

Elm Street

Forever Memories (Sara Lynn's)

Oakmont Avenue

A Clean Well-Lit Shop

Dot's Ice Cream Palace

Greg Langston's Pottery Shop

Custom Card Creations (Jennifer's)

Rebel Road

To Sara Lynn's

Crestview Road

King Street

Lake Drive

Hurley's Pub

To Bradford's

Rebel Lake

Rebel Forge, VA

To Jennifer's New Apartment

Chapter 1

For Eliza Glade's entire life, she somehow always managed to steal the spotlight from my sister and me, and wouldn't you know it, she kept her record perfect, even in death.

"You look absolutely radiant," I told my aunt Lillian, who was elegantly dressed in a formal evening gown. She's more than my aunt, though—Lillian is also my only employee at Custom Card Creations. My name's Jennifer Shane, and I own the shop of my dreams, a little handcrafted-card store tucked away on one end of Oakmont Avenue in the heart of Rebel Forge, Virginia. It's a place where customers can select one of our own handmade cards, or buy the materials to make one themselves.

After Lillian and I had worked at the store all day, we'd changed into more formal attire, and now we were ready to attend the chamber of commerce's annual awards banquet. The organization had held the ritual religiously for the past sixty-seven years, but it was the first time I'd been eligible to attend. The dinner was slated for Hurley's Pub, an easy walk from the store and a place I'd been many times.

Lillian was wearing an evening gown made of a rich material that was so sheer, it was nearly translucent.

The emerald green tint of the dress complemented her richly hennaed hair, and I'd never felt so dowdy in my thirty-something years of life. While my aunt was petite and graceful, I tended to feel big-boned and gawky, and it was never so obvious than when we were both dressed up.

"You look lovely as well," Lillian said. After casting a critical glance at my simple black dress, she added, "Though I do wish you'd let me treat you to a new outfit sometime." Lillian paused, then added enthusiastically, "I've got a wonderful idea, Jennifer. Why don't we go to Richmond in the morning, shop all day and then eat somewhere delightful tomorrow night? I know the most charming place we could stay, and we'd be back in time for lunch the next day. What do you say? I'd be delighted to pay." With seven ex-husbands and a shrewd mind for investing, Lillian could easily afford the gracious gesture. She worked at my shop for materials and instruction in lieu of a salary, and to my delight, my aunt had grown to love making cards nearly as much as I did.

"I'm tempted to take you up on it sometime, but you know I can't afford to close the card shop that long."

She waved a hand in the air, dismissing my protest. "Yes, I know how thoroughly wed you are to your business. Speaking of marriage, I'm still not certain you should have invited me as your guest to this banquet. Surely you could have found a suitable young man to escort you."

I wasn't about to have that conversation with her again. I hugged my aunt and said, "We both know that I probably wouldn't still be in business without your help. There's no way I could have asked anyone else tonight."

She raised an eyebrow in consternation, a look my

aunt had perfected from a great deal of practice over the years. "At least promise me you'll find some time to chat with the eligible young men there. Will Greg be attending?"

Greg Langston was my two-time former fiancé, but never my husband. He ran a pottery shop a few doors down from Custom Card Creations, and we were just starting to manage the awkwardness inherent in our proximity. Lillian had a dream that we'd make the third time a charm someday, and I was getting tired of trying to rid her of her delusions. "I suspect so, but I really don't know. We quit coordinating our social calendars a long time ago."

There must have been something in my voice that told her I was through talking about it. "Shall we go then?" she asked.

"Just let me lock up and I'll be ready."

As I secured the last dead bolt on the shop's front door, I heard my sister's voice calling me from up the street. "Jennifer, wait for me."

Sara Lynn had been cut from the same cloth as my aunt, the only two petite people in our family. She ran Forever Memories, a scrapbooking shop that had inadvertently led me to custom card making. I'd been her employee there not so long ago, and when Sara Lynn had rejected my idea of a card-making corner, I'd gone out on my own to prove there was a market for handcrafted cards in our resort community. Our brother, Bradford, was the sheriff for Rebel Forge, though at times it seemed his main duty was keeping our family together.

"You look award-winning," I said, appreciating the effort my sister had gone to. Sara Lynn normally eschewed makeup and fancy formal wear, but she was now skillfully enhanced from her brand-new hairdo all the way down to her expensive pumps.

"It's nonsense, and we all know it," Sara Lynn said. It was rumored around town that Sara Lynn was slated to receive the Rebel Forge Businessperson of the Year award, something that she'd yet to receive in all her years as a small-businesswoman. The reason for the slight was obvious: there was bad blood between my sister and Eliza Glade, the woman who ran the chamber—along with her businesses—with a velvet fist. However, it appeared that it was finally going to be Sara Lynn's turn—and she was long past due, in my opinion.

I looked behind her and asked, "Hey, where's Bailey?" Sara Lynn and her husband had been having marital troubles for months, but I had expected him to at least show up for his wife's crowning triumph. The Bippy—as we affectionately called the award—was the Oscar, Emmy and Obie combined for the folks who ran businesses in Rebel Forge, and I knew that, despite my sister's protests to the contrary, Sara Lynn had a place ready for the small golden anvil in the display behind her checkout counter.

"He's not coming," Sara Lynn snapped. From the tone of her voice, it was pretty obvious she was finished with that particular conversation.

Not that Lillian was going to accept the dismissal. "When are you going to kick him to the curb like he deserves?"

I was shocked by the harshness of my aunt's comment. "Lillian, that's out of line, even for you."

Our aunt was prepared to protest when Sara Lynn put a hand on my arm. "She's right, Jennifer." She took a deep breath, let it slowly out, then said, "You'll hear about this sooner or later, so it might as well be from me. Bailey and I have decided to split up."

I couldn't believe it. They'd been married forever,

and while I knew they'd had their share of problems, I never imagined it would come to this. "Sara Lynn, it will all work out. I just know you two are meant to be together."

She touched my shoulder lightly. "Thank you, Jennifer, but I don't think so."

Lillian nodded her obvious approval. "You had every right to toss him out after what he did."

"What happened?" I asked. "Is there something I don't know about?"

Sara Lynn frowned. "If you haven't heard the rumors yet, you will tonight. Bailey and I are completely and utterly finished. I could have probably forgiven him having an affair—I know he's just human—but I will never be able to get the image out of my mind of him in Eliza Glade's embrace."

I was shocked by the admission, but Lillian just nodded and said, "We're both here for you. You know that, don't you?"

I finally managed to find my voice. "Are you positive you want to go to the banquet tonight? Eliza's going to be making the presentation." I couldn't imagine my sister onstage with her worst enemy in the world. I turned to our aunt and asked, "Lillian, does your offer of a shopping trip to Richmond still stand? Let's go right now. What do you say, Sara Lynn? We'll have a blast."

"That's an excellent idea," Lillian said. "The three Shane women loose in the capital city. Let's do it."

Sara Lynn stood her ground, though. "I won't let that woman deprive me of this evening. I did nothing wrong, and I won't scuttle away to a corner and hide. Now, are you two coming or not? There's a banquet I'm determined to attend."

Behind Sara Lynn's back, Lillian looked questioningly at me, and I nodded to signal my acceptance. If Sara Lynn still wanted to go, then I would be right there beside her.

"Let's go," I said, with as much enthusiasm as I could muster.

As we walked to Hurley's Pub, the three of us chatted about the weather, the mutual states of our businesses, and just about everything but Sara Lynn's husband and his new paramour. I thought of myself as a strong woman, but I couldn't touch my sister's grit and determination. She was right, of course. The best way to handle the gossip and the scandal in our small town was to face it head on. That had always been her approach to life, and I'd constantly done my best to emulate her behavior, with varying degrees of success over the years.

Hurley's was closed to the public for the night, and the second we walked in I could see why. Jack Hurley had opened up the dividers between the dining areas, making his restaurant one big open space. There was a temporary stage set up in front, with a pair of tables split by a podium. Several people were mingling around the room, sharing drinks and quips, when we walked in. Was it my imagination, or was there a momentary hush throughout the room when everyone realized that Sara Lynn was there? I looked over at my sister, her head held high and her gaze unflinching, and I couldn't ever remember being more proud of her than I was at that moment. In less than a second, the crowd went back to their drinks and previous conversations, and I squeezed Sara Lynn's hand. "You are probably the bravest woman I know."

She shook her head briefly, but I could see that she was trying her best not to show any emotion at all. "Nonsense. I have every right to be here." As she spoke, I saw someone approaching us out of the corner of my eye. The relief I'd felt in seeing someone join us dissipated in an instant when I realized who it was.

Eliza Glade was heading our way, and it wasn't my imagination this time. The room was as quiet as a soft kiss; everyone there was holding their breath. Eliza wore a red dress that showed just a little bit too much of her voluptuous figure for a chamber of commerce dinner. Her blond hair had been teased and sprayed, and her makeup was more than just a smidge overdone. Truthfully, she looked like she would have been more at home in a Las Vegas lounge than Rebel Forge.

Before Eliza could reach my sister, Lillian disengaged from us and headed straight for the woman, effectively cutting her off from us. They shared a few whispered comments, then Lillian said something that rocked Eliza in her tracks. Her face reddened as if she'd been slapped, and I saw her back quickly away.

When Lillian rejoined us, there was a look of smug satisfaction on her face.

Sara Lynn said, "I don't need you to fight my battles for me. I'm perfectly capable of handling that woman myself."

Lillian just laughed. "What, and let you have all the fun? That's hardly fair."

"What did you say to her?" I asked. "You must have really spanked her hard."

"Me?" Lillian asked, her tone as innocent as she could summon. "I don't know what you're talking about."

Sara Lynn said, "Let's find our table, shall we? I don't relish having this crowd stare at me just standing here."

Lillian took her arm. "That's a capital idea. Let's see where the shrew has seated us."

We found our table, nearly concealed in a niche in back behind one of the few posts blocking the view of the stage. I was about to complain when I noticed that our tablemates were already there. It appeared that Sara Lynn, Lillian and I weren't the only Rebel Forge residents on Eliza's defecation roster. Savannah and Pete Jones, owners of The Lunch Box—a place where Lillian and I often ate—were already there.

"Hi, all," I said. "Where's Charlie?"

Charlie was their teenaged daughter and part-time waitress.

Savannah said, "She's off with some boy, if you can imagine that. I told that girl she has to stay focused if she wants to be a doctor, but does she listen to me?"

Pete, usually a man of few words, surprised us all by saying, "Savannah, the girl's got a right to a life of her own."

"I'm not trying to tell her what to do," Savannah said sharply, then noticed Lillian's grin. "What are you smiling about?"

The two of them had been friends from the cradle, and they weren't afraid to speak plainly to each other. Lillian said, "Your husband doesn't say much, but when he does talk, it might be a good idea to listen to him."

Savannah's features clouded up, but Lillian's smile never changed. After a long seven seconds, Savannah reluctantly laughed, and the rest of us joined in. "You might just have a point," she added, then looked at her husband. "Don't think you won this argument," she said.

"No, ma'am," Pete said, the smile still broad on his face.

Savannah said, "Now how in the world are they going to ever serve us if you three don't sit down? I don't get to eat out much, and I'm eager to try some of Jack Hurley's fare.''

We sat with them at the table, and I looked down at the place settings. Besides the knife, spoon and two forks, there was a pewter letter opener with an anvil at the end of the handle.

"How lovely," I said as I picked mine up and felt the solid heft of it.

Savannah smiled. "I'll say this for the award committee, they always have nice souvenirs. Sara Lynn, is that your husband over there trying to get your attention?"

We all turned to see Bailey waving frantically at my sister.

Lillian started to get up, but Sara Lynn beat her to it. "You sit tight. I'll take care of him. This is one battle I'll fight myself."

She left the table and headed directly for her husband. The last thing I wanted to hear was a shouting match between the two of them, but then I saw Sara Lynn drag him into the kitchen and out of earshot.

Savannah said softly, "There's trouble there."

"More than you know," Lillian confirmed. She looked around the room, then said, "There's a good turnout tonight, isn't there?"

Savannah nodded. "I think half of them are here to see that niece of yours onstage with Eliza."

"Don't say that in front of Sara Lynn," Lillian said.

"I'm not about to," Savannah said. She looked at Lillian, then said, "I hate to admit it, but you clean up pretty good."

Lillian laughed. "I was just about to say the same thing about you." She turned to Pete and said, "You look rather handsome yourself."

"Thank you, ma'am," Pete said. "I think you look nice, too."

Lillian clapped her hands. "Why you sly old dog, you. Pete Jones, are you turning into a talker on us?"

Pete shook his head, but I could see that he was smiling, caught up in the excitement of getting out of his kitchen, if only for one evening.

They were just starting to serve when Sara Lynn rejoined us, without her husband in tow.

"Are you all right?" I asked her. My sister looked more shaken than I'd ever seen her.

She didn't answer, but it was clear that further conversation wouldn't be welcome. We all managed to talk around her as the servers delivered our food. All I knew was that it must have been some kind of a confrontation to leave my sister shaking like she was.

After a pleasant meal of roast beef, asparagus tips in cheese sauce, and garlic mashed potatoes, our servers whisked our plates away and replaced them with chocolate mousses adorned with raspberries.

Lillian studied hers and said, "I'm so full, I don't think I can eat this."

I started to reach for her dessert plate before she could finish her sentence. "I'll be glad to help you out with it."

She swatted my hand, and the entire table laughed. "If I can't handle it, you'll be the first to know," Lillian said.

I dug into mine, regretting the richness of the dessert for just a second before I gave in to it. Jack had outdone himself, and I knew everyone at that dinner would be talking about the meal for weeks. I was just finishing my dessert when I felt someone approaching me from behind.

"Jennifer, may I have a word with you?"

It was Greg Langston, and he was wearing a tuxedo that made him look like a movie star. His tie perfectly matched his deep blue eyes, and his normally wild blond hair was tamed in place. I felt my heart skip despite the current state of our relationship, and I tried my best to keep my voice level as I answered. "I'll try to find time for you later. I'd offer you a seat, but we don't have any extras."

His hand brushed my shoulder, and I felt a tingle at his touch. "This is important."

I started to ask him what his definition of important was when Savannah nudged my elbow. "Girl, go talk to him. Don't worry, we'll save your seat."

I rolled my eyes at her, then stood up and faced him. "What is it, Greg?"

"Can we step away from the tables and talk about it?" he asked in that soft voice he'd always used to get to me.

Be strong, I told myself as I nodded my acceptance. Greg and I might have looked like a perfect match on paper, but we were constantly out of sync, and I couldn't imagine things getting any better between us. I was fully prepared to tell him no again, because I could see in his eyes that he was going to ask me out. My speech was all ready to deliver when he blurted out, "I'm seeing someone new—someone important to me—and I didn't want you to hear it from somebody else first."

"You don't have to keep me informed about the details of your love life," I said, just a little harsher than I'd intended.

He started to frown, then said, "Jennifer, I just thought you should know. I waited for you as long as I could, but I never seemed to get anywhere with you."

"Greg, I'm sorry, but there was just no way it was ever going to work out for us." There, at least I'd been able to deliver part of the speech I'd been ready to give. While I had been sincere when I'd said that Greg and I didn't have a future together, I still wasn't all that sure I wanted him dating other people. My own skewed sense of logic didn't have to make sense to anybody else. It was just the way I felt.

I saw an attractive blonde staring at us, tall and slim and rather elegant in a dress that perfectly matched Greg's tie. "You brought her here, didn't you?" I asked.

Greg looked over his shoulder, then waved to the young woman in question. "Jen, you intimidate the daylights out of her. It was all I could do to convince her to let me come over here and talk to you."

I studied her again, then offered her a friendly smile I didn't feel. *I* intimidated *her*? I sincerely doubted that. I knew I was cute enough, but no one would ever mistake me for the beauty he was with.

"Tell her she doesn't have anything to worry about from me," I said, then to my surprise, I saw her start toward us. Suddenly my friendly smile wasn't all that friendly any more.

Before I could make my retreat, she approached and offered a slender hand to me. "Hi. You must be Jennifer. It's such a pleasure to meet you."

"You, too," I said, barely managing not to mumble.

Greg said, "Jen, this is Stephanie Staunton."

I managed to nod as I heard a tapping on the microphone on the stage. My friend Grady Farrar—who ran the best hardware store in seven counties—was trying to get everyone's attention. "If you don't mind, could everyone take their seats?"

Greg and Stephanie returned to their prime position while I rejoined my table in the back of the room.

Savannah said, "That did not look good, Jennifer."

"If it's any consolation, it was worse than it appeared."

Lillian patted my hand, but I couldn't meet anyone's gaze. As I pretended to study the place settings, I noticed that though there were five of us sitting there, there were only four letter openers on the table. Funny, I was certain there had been five there when we'd first sat down.

My attention returned to Grady as he asked the audience, "Has anyone seen Eliza Glade? Eliza, are you out there?"

There were a few mutters from the crowd, but no Eliza. That was extremely odd, since I knew Eliza lived for her annual time in the spotlight.

Grady tugged on the lapels of his suit, whose fashion had last been stylish in the fifties, then said, "I guess that leaves it to me to do the honors."

He held up a small golden anvil, then said, "It's my pleasure to announce the winner of this year's award. Now I know Eliza's probably going to skin me alive for skipping her thirty-minute windup, but it's getting late and we all have businesses to run in the morning." That brought a chuckle from the crowd, and I could see that Grady was enjoying the attention. He'd been vice president forever, but from what he'd told me in the past, this was most likely the first time he'd ever been called on to speak.

"I'm going to read the name in this envelope, then we'll hear from the winner and that will wrap up our evening."

He tore the envelope open, and the look of surprise on his face was undeniable. It appeared that he wasn't quite able to believe it, but finally he held open the letter inside the envelope and read it aloud. "This year's winner has proven that youth does not necessarily mean unproven ability. Our recipient took a sound idea, and despite heavy opposition from her employer—a woman who should have known better, I might add—she made a success out of something her sister proclaimed publicly would never work. This year's winner of the Rebel Forge Businessperson of the Year award is Jennifer Shane."

I couldn't believe I'd just heard my name called, even as Savannah tried to propel me out of my seat. I whispered to my sister, "Sara Lynn, it's a mistake. It should be you."

Sara Lynn shook her head. "Nonsense. I can't stand the witch, but she's right. You made something work that I thought would fail from the start. Go get your award."

Lillian said, "Go on, Jennifer. You deserve it. No one else in the world knows how hard you've worked for it."

I stood, then started walking toward the front of the room. When I looked over at Greg, I saw that he was deep in conversation with Stephanie. I would have liked to see his smile, if just for a second, but he was otherwise engaged.

I was three steps from the raised platform, finally believing that it was indeed true that I'd won, when I heard a scream coming from the kitchen.

"She's dead!" the woman's voice shouted. "Someone stabbed her in the heart."

And that's when all hell broke loose.

Chapter 2

I stood there in shock, not sure what to do, and then, for some irrational reason, I turned and searched the crowd for the women at my table. Even though I knew I'd just left them, I had to be sure that Sara Lynn, Lillian and Savannah were all right. There was bedlam throughout the room—everyone was out of their seats and trying to all talk at once—but I managed to catch sight of Lillian holding onto Sara Lynn. That left Savannah, and in a moment of panic I couldn't see her. Then the crowd parted for just a moment and I found her sitting with her husband, Pete's arms around her. Ten seconds ago we'd been a calm group of adults sharing a lovely meal, and suddenly we were a mob.

I heard the sharp blast of a whistle cut through the chaos, and then another, and yet another. Bradford must have been close by to respond as quickly as he did. He cut through the crowd—coming from the kitchen where the scream had emanated—handsome and imposing in his sheriff's uniform, and as he took the stage, he said in a loud voice, "I need everyone to be quiet and sit back down."

There were a few people muttering in conversation before everyone finally did as they were told. My brother was well respected in Rebel Forge, and he wielded his influence in that room like a club.

After everyone was seated, Bradford said, "Now I need you all to cooperate. We're going to find out what's going on, but it's going to take a little time, so I'm asking for your patience."

"Who was stabbed?" a voice asked from the audience.

"Is she dead?" someone else asked.

Bradford held up his hands, then said, "When it's time to answer your questions, I will. For the moment, I need you all to cooperate and let me and my people do our jobs."

He went back into the kitchen, but I noticed not every cop followed him. There was a new man in uniform I didn't recognize guarding the door. Bradford had been forced to fire one of the men on his force. I'd been lobbying him to hire a woman to replace him, but my brother had told me he'd hire the best available candidate, and then he'd made a crack about me sticking to greeting cards and leaving the law enforcement to him. My brother wasn't a chauvinist, not by any means, but I still thought he could use a nudge in the right direction now and then. He'd thought otherwise.

I started back to my seat when the new deputy called out, "Ma'am, you need to sit down."

"I'm trying to," I said. "My table is back there."

"Just find an empty chair," he snapped.

I ignored him and headed back to my group anyway. If he thought that snarling tone of voice was going to work on me, he was mistaken. I couldn't believe it when he started toward me, and without meaning to, I scampered back to my original seat and sat down, as if we were playing musical chairs and it was the last one available.

He kept coming, and loomed over me. "Am I going to have trouble from you?"

Lillian butted in, as was her nature. "If you don't, you'll be the first man in her life to make that claim." She stuck out her hand. "I'm Lillian. You must be new."

He wanted to scold me more, I could see it in his eyes, but Lillian had defused the tension. "I'm Hank," he admitted as he took her hand.

"How delightful to meet you. These are my nieces Jennifer and Sara Lynn, and these are my dear friends, Savannah and Peter Jones."

He tipped his chin down for a moment. "Nice to meet you folks. Now I'd better get back to the door." Hank stared at me a second longer before he left, as if challenging me to say anything or move an inch off my chair, and for a moment I was tempted to do both. Then I remembered that Bradford was back in the kitchen investigating a murder, and it was no time to have a tantrum.

When he saw that I was going to behave myself, Hank turned his back to me and walked to his former station by the door.

He was barely out of earshot when Lillian said, "My, he's awfully cute, isn't he?"

I stared openly at my aunt. "You're kidding, right? I thought he was going to handcuff me for a minute there. What a jerk."

"Jennifer, you've got to be a little more relaxed with your standards if you're ever going to meet anyone new."

I couldn't believe Lillian was trying to discuss my love life after what had just happened. "Can we put my personal life on hold for the moment? I wonder who was stabbed. What an awful scream."

Savannah nodded. "It was terrible, all right. Who would do such a thing right here with everyone around?"

Sara Lynn was strangely quiet.

I looked at her a second, then asked, "Are you all right?"

"No, but I will be."

I was still trying to figure out exactly what she meant by that when Bradford came back out of the kitchen. He was pelted with questions as he made his way to the stage, but he didn't answer any of them until he was at the microphone.

My brother said, "I'm going to ask you all a few questions, then I need you to file out one at a time and give my deputies your names, addresses and telephone numbers. Please cooperate with us and do as I ask."

"So who was stabbed?" the same voice from before called out, and there were several mutters from the crowd.

I could see Bradford considering the possibilities, but he knew Rebel Forge better than anybody else in town, and I had to believe he realized it would be impossible to keep the lid on the name of the murder victim past midnight.

Bradford stared at the crowd, then finally said, "The victim was Eliza Glade, but I'd appreciate it if you'd wait to spread the word until we can get in touch with her mother over in Louisa."

That started another wave of discussion, but Bradford managed to kill it pretty fast. "The only reason I told you this right now is that I need to see everyone who talked with her or saw her this evening to come forward to the stage so I can interview you."

Everybody started to get up when Bradford added, "Okay, let's try this a different way. Keep standing until I eliminate you. Was there anybody who saw Eliza after the meal?"

Nobody admitted as much, and Bradford went on. "Okay, did anyone actually talk to her this evening?"

In a loud, clear voice, Lillian said, "I did."

Bradford bit his lip, no doubt expecting something just like that from our aunt. The two of them hadn't gotten along for twenty years, and I could tell my brother wasn't surprised by her admission. "Come on up and I'll talk to you in a minute. Is there anyone else?"

A few people raised their hands, and Bradford motioned for them to join him. I was waiting for him to dismiss us when Beth Anderson, a waitress at Hurley's who sported multitinted hair, pointed at Sara Lynn and said, "You talked to her. I saw it."

"She did not," I said. "I was standing right beside her, and Lillian cut Eliza off before she could get to us."

Beth shook her head. "I'm not talking about that. I saw her arguing with that woman in the kitchen."

There were shocked murmurs throughout the crowd, and Sara Lynn said, "We had a few words, but it was nothing."

It was pretty obvious Bradford didn't want to call Sara Lynn to the front, but he had no choice. I started forward, when he added, "Don't tell me you talked to her, too, Jennifer."

"I didn't, but I'm coming anyway."

Bradford shook his head. "If I need you, you'll be the first to know. Does anyone else have anything to say?"

Nobody volunteered anything, so Bradford said, "Then I'll ask you all to leave. Be patient with us, folks, we're doing the best we can. And thanks for cooperating."

As everyone else started to get in line at the rear door, I followed Sara Lynn up to the front. Hank stepped in and said, "You heard the sheriff. You need to go."

I gave him my hardest look, then said, "If you think you can stop me, you'd better get your gun, because you'll have to shoot me to get me to leave my sister's side."

Sara Lynn said numbly, "It's all right, Jennifer. I'll be fine."

"I know you will. I'm going to be right by your side," I said.

We were at a stalemate when Bradford approached. "What's the problem here?"

Hank turned to him and said, "She won't leave."

"Why am I not surprised? Hank, have you met my family?"

He nodded, but didn't say a word.

Bradford shook his head as he looked at me, then finally said, "Come on, I don't have the energy to fight with you tonight." He turned to his deputy. "Help Jody at the door, will you?"

Hank nodded, then said, "Listen, I'm sorry if I stepped over the line, but you said—"

Bradford patted his shoulder. "You did exactly the right thing."

After he was gone, Bradford looked at Sara Lynn and me and said, "You might as well come up front. Let's get this over with."

As we followed Bradford, I whispered to my sister, "Did you really see her in the kitchen? What happened?" I couldn't imagine Sara Lynn and Eliza together in the close confines of the kitchen. An unwelcome thought came as I fought not to add, without blood being shed.

Bradford stopped and looked at me before Sara Lynn could answer. "If you don't mind, I'd like to interview the witnesses myself without your assistance."

"Fine," I said. "I was just asking."

There were seven people standing in front of the room, including Beth. She approached Sara Lynn before Bradford could say anything. "I'm so sorry I told on you."

She looked like she was going to start crying, and my sister patted her hand. "You did the right thing, dear. I have nothing to hide."

That obviously made Beth feel better, and she started back toward the kitchen.

Bradford stopped her dead in her tracks. "Where are you going?"

"I have to help clean up," Beth explained.

Bradford shook his head. "I'm afraid they'll have to get along without you for now. I need you here."

"I already told you what I saw," Beth said.

"Have a seat," he said, pointing to an empty table in front. "I'm not finished with you yet."

Beth didn't look happy about the command, but she followed it nonetheless. My brother was a hard man for most folks to say no to, though I hadn't had much trouble over the years. Still, I could see how he could be intimidating with that cold stare and booming voice.

I could see him glance between Sara Lynn and Lillian, so I wasn't really surprised when he tapped my sister first. "Come on, Sis."

Sara Lynn followed him, and I started after him when Lillian touched my arm. "Let your brother do his job," she said to me.

Bradford looked startled by the defense as he nodded his thanks. "It will go faster if you wait right here, Jennifer."

I reluctantly agreed as I watched my brother escort my sister off for questioning in a murder case. It was not a scene I'd ever imagined I'd witness.

I turned to Lillian after they were gone. "What exactly did you say to Eliza when she started toward us before dinner?"

Lillian shook her head, refusing to answer.

"Come on," I said. "You're not going to tell me?"

"Jennifer, I don't want to get you into trouble with your brother. Besides, it was nothing."

I knew better than that. Lillian had scored a direct hit with Eliza; the stricken look on the woman's face testified to that.

"You're going to have to tell Bradford. Why not tell me?"

Lillian frowned. "Do you think I'm all that proud of the fact that one of the last things that woman heard in her life was my snippy remark about her low morals? Jennifer, I was wrong to confront her. It wasn't my fight, but I had to step in and be clever, and now I couldn't take it back even if I wanted to."

I knew Lillian had a certain sensitivity about her, but her brash nature usually made it hard to remember that all the time. "Listen, I'm sorry, I didn't mean to push you on it."

When Lillian looked at me, I could see a tear tracking down her left cheek. "Jennifer, it's fine, but I really don't want to talk about it right now, all right?"

"Certainly," I said, looking at the other witnesses gathered around the front of the room. Addie Mason, a tall, reedy woman with flaming red hair, was there. As Eliza's partner at Heaven Scent, it was understandable why she'd talked to the woman that evening. It kind of surprised me to see Luke Penwright there, though. Luke and Eliza had been married ten years before, but it had lasted less than six months before they'd split up. From what I'd heard around town, Luke had been trying unsuccessfully for years to get her back. He was good-looking enough in his own way, but there was something about his heavy eyebrows and constant scowl that always gave me the creeps. Polly Blackburn was waiting to speak with Bradford as well. I knew some folks in town called her Jolly Polly, but it wasn't from her disposition. The woman was nearly as wide as she was tall, and she had a tongue that could scorch the paint off the side of a barn from thirty feet. The only one left was Kaye Jansen. I didn't have a clue she'd even known Eliza.

I touched my aunt's arm, and whispered, "Did Kaye know Eliza very well?"

Lillian frowned, then said, "She knew her well enough to sue her for slander. Nothing ever came of it, but they weren't big fans of one another. I heard that it didn't help matters when Kaye's father-in-law hired Eliza to do their books. I can't imagine what they had to talk about tonight."

"Eliza and Polly didn't get along either, did they?"

Lillian said, "No, Polly always complained bitterly that she should be the chamber's president, but Eliza kept getting reelected year after year. From what I've heard, there were accusations of stuffed ballot boxes during more than one election."

I was about to ask about the others, since my aunt knew most of the skeletons hanging in Rebel Forge's closets, but Bradford broke up our conversation when he returned with Sara Lynn. "Lillian, I'll see you now." He turned to me and added, "Jennifer, do you mind taking Sis home with you? Sara Lynn doesn't need to be alone tonight."

"I'll do it," I said.

"I don't need a babysitter," my sister insisted.

"And you're not getting one. To be honest with you, I'm not crazy about staying home alone tonight myself."

Sara Lynn scowled. "You're never alone, Jennifer. You've always got your roommates."

"I doubt they'd be much comfort tonight." That wasn't fair to my cats, but I had to come up with an excuse to be with Sara Lynn. I doubted Oggie and Nash would even notice I was gone, as long as their meals came on time. I loved the little scoundrels, but there were times when I wondered if the feeling was mutual. "Let me just go by the apartment and feed them, then I'll come home with you."

Sara Lynn shook her head. "Jennifer, I have no desire to go back to my house tonight." She hesitated, then added, "It's too empty without Bailey there. I'll gladly take your couch instead."

"Nonsense, you can have the bed and I'll sleep out on the couch. It will be like camping."

She rolled her eyes at me. "Jennifer, you're nearly a foot taller than I am, and I barely fit on it. You would dangle over from both ends. I'll be fine."

We were still debating our sleeping arrangements when Lillian rejoined us. As Bradford called to Addie Mason, our aunt said, "Are you two still here?"

"We're trying to decide where we're going to sleep tonight," I said.

"I thought it would be obvious. You two are going to be my guests tonight." Lillian had a huge old house, and I knew she had plenty of room for guests, even though she'd converted one entire bedroom into a closet.

I could see Sara Lynn wasn't crazy about the idea, so I had to plow ahead. "We'd love to. I just have to feed Oggie and Nash first."

"By all means, bring them with you. You know how the rascals love to explore my house."

That was usually a sticking point with Lillian whenever I dared bring them over, but I wasn't about to argue with her. "They'll love it. Come on, Sara Lynn. It will be fun."

She raised an eyebrow, but she didn't back out of the arrangement, so I considered it a victory.

As we walked out of Hurley's, I noticed that Hank was watching us. My first reaction was to stick my tongue out at him, but I settled for an icy stare and an aloof manner. That would teach him to try to order me around. When I glanced back to see how my withering treatment had affected him, I realized he'd dismissed me and had moved on to the next person in his line. And I'd wasted a perfectly good freeze on him.

There was a chill in the mountain air with the sun long gone, and I wished for a moment I'd brought a sweater with me. Lillian chattered, "Let's hurry, my Mustang's in front of the shop. We can get your cars tomorrow."

As we hurried back to Custom Card Creations, Sara Lynn said, "Thanks, but I'm going home to collect a few things first. I'll need my car for that."

"I can take you," Lillian insisted.

"Blast it, woman, I'm not nine years old. I'm perfectly capable of going home alone."

Lillian smiled, and Sara Lynn couldn't let it go. "What are you grinning about?"

"I was afraid you'd lost your fire for a minute there, but I see you've found it."

Sara Lynn chuckled softly. "Don't kid yourself; I'm teetering on the edge."

"That's all the more reason you shouldn't be alone tonight," I said. "If you come with me to get my cats, I'll follow you home. Then we can go to Lillian's together." I looked at my aunt and said, "Do you have any dessert in your refrigerator? I've got a craving for chocolate."

"How about a pan of my famous double chocolate brownies?" Lillian asked.

"You've got some at home?" I said. "That would be perfect."

"I don't have them ready, but they will be by the time you two run your errands."

Sara Lynn said, "I don't want you to go to any trouble for us."

"Speak for yourself, Sis," I said. "Go to the trouble," I told Lillian.

Lillian laughed. "You really should come out of your shell more, Jennifer."

"What can I say? I'm trying."

We split up in front of the card shop, and soon we were at my converted attic loft. I had the top space of a charming old Victorian, and it was my favorite place I'd had in years, despite the presence of a forgetful poltergeist.

There was a note taped to my door, and I wondered if one of my downstairs neighbors was trying to make peace with me again. We'd had good reason to argue in the past, and I was in no mood for their antics.

It was from Hester Taylor, my landlord. I opened it and read,

> " 'Jennifer, I'm sorry I missed you. I'm selling the house and grounds, so I'm afraid you'll have to find somewhere else to live. I do apologize, but I have to do this. You can have one more week, but you've got to be gone by then.—Hester.' "

"How do you like that?" I said as I handed Sara Lynn the note.

"She can't do that," Sara Lynn said. "The woman's got to give you more notice than that."

"You're probably right, but I've never been keen on staying somewhere I'm not wanted. It looks like I'll be moving again."

"I've got an idea," Sara Lynn said. "You can move in with me. Now that Bailey's gone, I'd love the company."

"If it were just me, I might take you up on your offer," I said, lying with an innocent face. "But you know how the cats are. They would drive you nuts in no time." It was certainly true that Oggie and Nash weren't my sister's biggest fans, but it was by no means the only reason I'd refused her offer. I'd struggled too hard and too long to be out on my own and out of my family's formidable shadow, and I wasn't about to let one of them suck me back in. As soon as Lillian and Bradford found out I'd been evicted, I knew they'd get in line to offer me housing, so I had to be firm in my resolve from the beginning.

"Well, you can think about it," Sara Lynn said. "Just let me know if you change your mind."

"Thanks for the offer. I truly do appreciate it, but I'm not going to take you up on it."

As I walked in, the cats were sitting quietly on the sofa, one on either arm, as if they were statues awaiting my arrival. "Well, aren't you two looking particularly fine tonight?"

I swear they both looked at me like I'd lost my mind, an expression I'd grown used to from them. "I'm guessing you're ready for your snacks."

As I gave them a few treats, I said, "Guess what? We're going to stay at Lillian's tonight."

Oggie protested with a yowl and bolted from the room. I looked at Nash and asked, "Aren't you going to follow suit?"

I was ignored once again, so I took advantage of it and gathered up a few of my own things before putting them in their carriers. By the time I was ready to go, Sara Lynn had undoubtedly reconsidered her offer.

"You're probably right," she said as we walked out of the house. "I don't think your cats would enjoy my place."

"They appreciate your offer, though," I said. Lying to my sister was getting to be a habit tonight. My two bandits could not have cared less for my sister's generosity.

After I got the cats situated in the backseat of my Gremlin, we were ready to go. When we got to Sara Lynn's house, I hit the dome light and saw that both cats were sound asleep. Sometimes traveling in their carriers agitated them. When I was lucky, though, the motion of the car, coupled with the darkness, acted like a rocking bassinet on a baby and knocked them out cold. They were absolutely adorable, especially when they were sound asleep. I locked the car and joined Sara Lynn at her front door. It appeared that every light in her house was turned on, lighting it up like a luminaria at Christmas.

"Wow, I'd hate to see your electric bill this month," I said, then I looked at my sister. "Sara Lynn, what's wrong?"

"When I left here tonight, every light in the house was turned off."

Chapter 3

That was hard to imagine, given the current state of illumination. "Are you sure?"

She didn't even offer me a withering look—something that spoke volumes. "I'm positive."

"Could Bailey have come by after you two talked tonight at Hurley's?"

"No, he gave me his keys yesterday when he left. That was part of our arrangement. He isn't supposed to enter the house again unless I'm here."

I couldn't imagine Bailey defying her. My sister might have been petite, but she had a tongue sharp enough to wilt kudzu.

She hesitated, her key hovering near the lock. I put my hand on hers. "Listen, if you're worried about it, we can call Bradford. I'm sure he'll come right over."

Sara Lynn paused a moment, then said, "No, he's got enough to worry about tonight without trotting over here. I'm sure it's all perfectly innocent."

She unlocked her front door and pushed it in. I was right behind her, but I suddenly wished I'd brought my softball bat along with us for protection. It was amazing how the heft of that aluminum club could fill me with confidence. My sister wasn't empty-handed, though. As soon as the door was unlocked, she dove into her handbag and pulled out a vial of pepper spray with one hand and a stun gun with the other. Maybe I wouldn't need my bat after all.

For some reason I'd been expecting the living room to be trashed, as if the burglars had turned on every light in the house while they ransacked it. Instead, it was as neat as it had ever been, and I felt myself relax. Sara Lynn wasn't quite so trusting though. I followed my older sister from room to room until we were both satisfied that nothing had been touched and no one was lurking in a corner for us. It was pretty clear she was still troubled by the lights, but since nothing else appeared to have been disturbed, I was ready to write it off as one of her senior moments of forgetfulness. She went through the house, flipping switches off as she neatly packed an overnight bag, and we were at the door ready to leave when she said, "I need to check one more thing before we go."

"Sara Lynn, we looked under every bed and inside every closet. There's nobody here."

"Be patient, Jennifer, this will just take a second." She walked into the kitchen, so I followed her, curious to see what place she felt we'd ignored in our search. She stopped at her pantry—really nothing more than a small closet that wouldn't have hidden one of my cats, let alone the neatest burglar who'd ever hit Rebel Forge. Sara Lynn reached to the back of the top shelf and pulled out a cylinder of oatmeal.

"If you're hungry," I said, "Lillian's making brownies, remember?"

She ignored me and pulled off the canister's lid. To my surprise, Sara Lynn stuck her hand into the container, and after rooting around inside it for a few seconds, she pulled out a piece of paper. "Hey, I didn't know those things came with prizes."

Her face was grim as she read the paper, then she

handed it to me. It was Bailey's handwriting; there was no mistaking his sloppy printing.

"Sara Lynn, this is my IOU. I'll pay it all back, hopefully before you even realize it's gone. I'm sorry, about everything. —Bailey."

I handed it back to her. "What's this all about?"

"We've kept five hundred dollars in here for emergencies since we first got married. It was our agreement that we would never touch it unless there was a dire reason."

"So maybe Bailey had an emergency," I said, trying to ease my sister's troubled mind.

"Jennifer, you don't understand. We made it a ritual of each of us putting in half. Neither one of us was ever to take more than their share. I can't believe Bailey would be this petty."

I shrugged. "I can't explain it," I said. "But it's not going to do any good sitting here staring at the note. Let's go to Lillian's."

She nodded absently, threw the note onto the counter, then changed her mind and put it in her purse. "So why did he leave all the lights on if he came here just to take money?"

"For that matter," I said, "how did he get inside if he surrendered his keys to you?"

She shook her head. "I know one way." I followed her out onto the porch and watched as she stuck her hand into a flowerpot. After a minute of rooting around, she retrieved a key. "I'd forgotten all about this. He must have used it tonight to get in and take our emergency fund."

"Then why leave the lights on?" I asked.

"Who knows? Maybe he was in a hurry, or maybe

he was leaving me some kind of message. I just don't understand that man anymore."

I put my arm around Sara Lynn's shoulder. "Come on, let's get out of here. You'll feel better once we get to Lillian's. Would you like to leave your car here and ride with me?" My sister was shaken up, something that I'd seen only a few times in my life, and it had me worried.

"No, I'll be fine." Outside on the front walk, she looked back at the house, now dark throughout, then turned to her car. "Let's get out of here."

I followed her to Lillian's place, relieved once we were there. "Can I get one of the carriers for you?" Sara Lynn asked.

"No, they balance each other out. You could grab my bag for me, though."

Lillian must have been waiting at the door for us. She threw it open just as we reached it. "Hello, ladies. Jennifer, you're in the pink bedroom, and Sara Lynn, you're in the lavender one." For a relatively unconventional woman, my aunt enjoyed the softer color palettes when it came to decorating her house.

I put the carriers in the designated bedroom, then left their doors open, in case Oggie and Nash woke up and wanted a stretch. Lillian had set up a litter box in one corner, along with putting out some water and the treats both cats loved. I was impressed that my aunt had been so thorough, but then I realized that she was always the perfect hostess, no matter if her houseguests walked on two legs or four.

I found Lillian in the kitchen, and took in the delightful aroma of freshly baking brownies. "When will they be out of the oven?"

Lillian laughed. "Patience, Jennifer. They've got another five minutes of baking, and then I like to let them cool before I ice them."

"Well, I'd like to lose twenty pounds, but that's not

happening either. I'll give you five minutes to bake and five to cool, but that's my best offer."

Sara Lynn came out, and I noticed she held the note from Bailey clutched in her hand.

Before I could warn Lillian not to say anything, our aunt asked, "What's that you're holding so tightly?"

"It's a note from Bailey," Sara Lynn said simply.

"How sweet," she said, the sarcasm dripping from her words. "So he's already apologizing and trying to crawl back to you. I know how you feel about him, though I can't imagine why, but if you do take the cur back, I hope you're going to make it so miserable for him that he cries like a little girl."

Sara Lynn handed Lillian the note, then after she explained its meaning, she said, "Somehow I don't think this is a reconciliation attempt."

Lillian looked surprised by the admission. "Everyone knows I'm not Bailey's biggest fan, but it seems petty even for him, to rob you on his way out the door." She tapped the note with a finger, then said, "If that's what he did. Sara Lynn, when was the last time you saw that cash?"

She thought about it a few seconds, then said, "It's been months. I don't ordinarily keep tabs on my emergency fund. Every now and then I'll check on it, though, just to make sure it's there if I need it."

Lillian said, "Then how do you know he took it tonight? This note's not dated, is it?"

Sara Lynn took it back from her, studied it a few seconds, then said, "No, there's nothing here that would tell me he robbed us tonight, but somehow I know in my heart he did. Why else would all the lights be on in our house?"

Lillian shrugged. "Sorry, I don't have an answer for that. You'll just have to ask him the next time you see him."

The oven timer went off and Lillian said, "The brownies are ready." She opened the oven door and poked a toothpick into the center of the rich brown concoction. After seeing that it came out clean, Lillian pulled the pan out and put it on a cooling rack. "I'd like to wait an hour, but I insist we at least wait five minutes." She reset the timer, then put out plates of fine china, Waterford drinking goblets and linen napkins.

"You don't have to bring out your best for us," I said. "A paper plate and a plastic cup apiece would be fine."

Lillian arched one eyebrow as she looked at me. "Jennifer, how can it be a party if we treat it like it's so commonplace?"

Sara Lynn was still staring at the note when I looked over at her. There had to be some way to get my sister out of her funk. I thought furiously of all the things that had worked in the past, but none of them seemed appropriate tonight. Finally, I decided to let her have her silent introspection. After all, if Bailey really was gone, she had something worth mourning. While I wouldn't have been able to live with the man for more than fifteen minutes without wanting to beat him to death with his television remote control, he and Sara Lynn had found a happy balance in their lives together, and I knew my sister would be devastated by her marriage's demise no matter what the circumstances. I lifted my eyebrows as I looked at Lillian, hoping that she could make things better, but she just shrugged as the timer went off again. Putting on an air of false buoyancy, Lillian said, "It's time to indulge."

As she lifted crumbling fragments of brownie out of the pan, I was there with a knife, ready to slather on the frosting. The brownies were from a boxed mix and the icing was in a plastic container, but I didn't care. They smelled delicious, and besides, who had the time to make them from scratch anymore?

After Lillian had filled our plates and I had topped the brownies with an ample layer of milk chocolate icing, we took our treats to the table and sat down.

Our hostess said, "I'd offer you ice cream, but all I have at the moment is peach, and I'm not sure how it would go with our main course. Would anyone like coffee?"

"Not me," I said. "I want milk."

"Sara Lynn?" Lillian asked.

"Whatever you're having will be fine with me," she said absently.

Lillian and I did our best to make it a party, but Sara Lynn was only half there, and soon after we ate, she excused herself and went off to the lavender bedroom.

As I helped Lillian clean up, I asked, "Is there anything we can do for her? I hate seeing Sara Lynn like this."

Lillian said, "Goodness knows I've been through more than my fair share of divorces over the years. All I can say is they seem to get a little easier as you go along—not that that particular advice would do her much good right now. She's going to have to work her way through it by herself. All we can do is support her in any way we can."

As I rinsed the dishes Lillian washed in the sink, I said in a low voice, "Can you believe he robbed her on the way out?"

"So you don't think it could have happened months ago?"

"Lillian, it's a good story, but I'm not buying it.

Those lights were on for a reason. I'm betting that Bailey wanted her to know exactly what he was doing."

Lillian frowned as she handed me a glass. I hated the thought of dropping one, knowing that I couldn't afford to replace it without depleting the entire contents of my slim bank account.

"There's something we haven't considered," she finally said. "Maybe he needed it tonight to escape."

"Escape from what?" I asked. "A bad marriage? Five hundred bucks wouldn't help him do that."

"You're forgetting something, Jennifer. If Sara Lynn is right and Bailey was having an affair with Eliza, is it possible he killed her and needed the money to run away?"

I nearly dropped the glass I was rinsing. "Honestly, can you see Bailey murdering anyone?"

Lillian shrugged. "Some people have a surprising way of fooling those closest to them. If you hadn't heard it from Sara Lynn herself, could you ever have imagined Bailey would cheat on her, especially with Eliza Glade?"

I thought about it for nearly a minute before I spoke. "No, it's still hard for me to believe, but I once heard Bradford say that given the right circumstances, anyone could commit murder."

"I believe it," Lillian said.

"You honestly think Bailey could have done it?" I couldn't imagine my brother-in-law displaying anything that resembled that kind of passion or anger.

"I'm not just talking about him anymore," Lillian said as her gaze drifted back toward the lavender bedroom.

I was just glad I didn't have anything in my hands at the time or I would have surely dropped it. "You're not suggesting Sara Lynn killed her, are you? I don't believe it—not for a second."

"Calm down, Jennifer, I don't believe it either. But your brother is going to have to consider the possibility, whether she's related to him or not. Sara Lynn is going to be under his microscope, and so is Bailey."

"Then the two of us have to figure out who really killed Eliza," I said resolutely.

"Surely your brother is capable of doing that himself," Lillian protested.

"He is, but how long will Sara Lynn's reputation last if Bradford doesn't wrap this up quickly? Her business could die before the truth comes out, if there's a suspicion that she's a murderer. We can't let that happen. We have to uncover the truth, and we have to do it quickly."

"I'm in," Lillian said as we finished the dishes. "But where do we start?"

"Let's make a list of who had a reason to want Eliza dead," I said, then hastily added, "besides my sister and her husband, that is."

"We can skip them for now," Lillian agreed, "but that doesn't mean we can just forget about them."

"I don't want to talk about that," I said, unwilling to accept the possibility that Sara Lynn, or even Bailey, could be a murderer. That was, along with a thousand other reasons, why I would have made a terrible cop. I let my emotions influence my thought process too much. Honestly, though, I wouldn't have had it any other way.

Lillian looked around, then said, "I wish I had our white board from the store. It's so much easier when we can see our ideas printed out. Wait a second, I've got an idea."

She left me for a minute, and I stayed right where

I was. With everything that had happened today, I hadn't had time to dwell on my own problems. Thanks to my nutty landlord, I was going to have to find a new place to live. The fact that Hester was also evicting my neighbors Barrett and Jeffrey didn't help, though the two of them had found their own ways to make my life less than idyllic. So where could I go? I knew Lillian would take me in, but we spent enough time together at the card shop. I doubted either one of us could take cohabitating as well. Bradford and his family would give me a place to sleep, but I'd fought most of my life to get out on my own, and I wasn't going to surrender it so easily. I'd find a place again. After all, I had some time. How hard could it be?

Lillian came back in with a large mirror and an eyeliner. "Have you completely lost your mind?" I asked.

"Hey, I've left many a message this way in the past. Most of my ex-husbands found it charming."

"I just bet they did," I said.

Lillian wrote SUSPECT, MOTIVE, MEANS, and OPPORTUNITY on the mirror. Below those, she listed the names of the people my brother had talked to tonight. I knew there could be more suspects than that, but we had to somehow limit our list to less than the telephone book for all of Rebel Forge. She wrote the names Addie Mason, Luke Penwright, Polly Blackburn and Kaye Jansen down the left side of the mirror.

I nodded as she worked. "So we're looking at everyone who admitted to seeing Eliza tonight."

"Yes, but I'm missing someone," Lillian said as she studied the list.

"Beth Anderson?" I asked, half in jest.

"Exactly," Lillian said.

As she added the waitress's name, I said, "I wasn't serious. What possible reason would she have to kill Eliza?"

Lillian refused to strike the name. "Don't be so naïve, Jennifer. Eliza could make an enemy faster than Stephen King can give you nightmares. We shouldn't cross her off our list until we can prove she's innocent."

"Then let's see what we do know," I said. "Let's take Addie. Can you honestly see her killing Eliza? They've been partners for years."

"What better reason could she have?" Lillian said. "That woman would drive a saint to murder. I wonder what happens to Eliza's share of Heaven Scent now that she's dead."

I shrugged. "I'd think it would go to her estate."

"Don't be so hasty in that assumption," Lillian said. "A lot of partners leave their stake in their companies to their co-owners so the business can keep on operating. We need to look into that."

"And how do you propose we do that?" My aunt had an underground network of sources and information that would have astounded Bradford, but I didn't see how she could find that out.

"We're simply going to ask her," Lillian said. "I think we should pay her a social call after work tomorrow to give her our sympathies in losing her business partner. You can make her a lovely card, and it will be the perfect excuse to deliver it."

"You could make her one yourself," I said.

Lillian frowned. "I doubt she'd appreciate my humor. This calls for a more conventional card than my offerings. One of yours would be perfect." I'd encouraged Lillian to indulge her wicked sense of humor and start her own card corner in my shop. While her dark sentiments weren't appropriate for everyone who came into the card shop, she certainly had developed a rather loyal fan base for her wit.

"You're probably right," I said. "But I can't do it

after work. I'm having dinner with Gail and her new boyfriend." Gail was my best friend in the world. I couldn't imagine my life without her in it.

"Just the three of you?" Lillian asked. "How cozy."

I'd been avoiding telling my aunt about my dinner plans for tomorrow night, but it was time to get it over with. "Actually, Gail's boyfriend, Reggie, is inviting an old college roommate to be my dinner companion. We're going to his mother's house in High Meadows."

"That's so very cosmopolitan of you. Very well, if we can't do it after work, we'll take a long lunch and close the card shop."

I stared at my aunt, not able to believe that she was letting me off the hook that easily. "That's it? No third degree? I expected at least a water torture to pry more details from me."

"Please, Jennifer, your social schedule isn't all that great a concern to me."

"Since when?" I asked. She'd done everything in her power to fix me up with an eligible young man, and now suddenly she was backing off. What was going on here?

"Don't flatter yourself, child. I've got more important things to think about." She tapped the next name on our list. "Luke was there tonight, though I didn't realize he was a member of the chamber. I wonder how he managed an invitation. Or did he just crash the party to see Eliza?"

"Bradford will find out," I said, confident in my brother's abilities to follow all of the orthodox clues. He came up a little short sometimes only when the killer used real imagination—something he assured me was rarer in reality than the mysteries I liked to read.

Lillian frowned, then asked, "Why would he kill her, though? I've been under the impression that for some unfathomable reason, the man was still in love with his ex-wife."

"Don't you think any of your exes are pining away for you?" I asked, only half joking. My aunt could cast a spell on a man that made him lose his senses completely.

"I'd be terribly disappointed if any of them have gotten over me," she said with an utterly straight face.

"So he wouldn't kill her," I said. "Not while he still had hope."

"But did he? Eliza was seeing Bailey. Perhaps Luke took that as a threat."

I shook my head. "That might explain it if Bailey was the victim, but not Eliza."

Lillian frowned. "We'll come back to him later, then."

She moved her pencil to the next names on the list. "Polly and Kaye both hated her, but did either one of them despise the woman enough to drive a letter opener into Eliza's chest? That speaks of a certain level of passion I have difficulty seeing either one of them attain."

I thought about what I knew of the women in question. Polly had visited the card shop twice since we'd opened, and though I'd tried to entice her to try her hand at crafting her own cards, she'd opted both times for a ready-made offering. While I enjoyed the profit margin of selling cards Lillian and I made, I was always proselytizing, trying to share just how much fun card making was with my clientele. She'd flatly refused, though, so I'd dropped the matter. As for Kaye, while she hadn't been in my shop, she had visited Sara Lynn's a time or two when I'd worked there. I'd found the woman abrupt and condescending, but I didn't know if I could see her as a murderer.

"So what do we do next?" I asked, as Sara Lynn walked out in her pajamas and a robe.

At least the back of the mirror faced her, and not the front. I sprayed the glass with some cleaner Lillian had brought out to correct any mistakes we might make, and then wiped away the evidence of our notes with a paper towel as Sara Lynn approached. She noticed me working on the mirror and said, "It's a little late for housecleaning, isn't it?"

"I just wanted to touch it up a little," I said as I handed the glass cleaner back to Lillian. "There, I think that got it. Thanks, that smudge was bugging me."

Lillian laughed, and though I could tell it was forced, I wasn't sure Sara Lynn could. Working closely with my aunt over the past several months had taught me the nuances of her actions and tones of voice better than I'd ever learned around her in the past. "I'm hoping Jennifer finds something unsettling about the hall carpet. I've been meaning to run the vacuum for the past three days, but I just never manage to get around to it."

She'd been teasing, but Sara Lynn was a demon of a cleaner. "Is your vacuum still in the closet over there?"

"Dear, I was just trying to be amusing. Failing at it, too, I might add."

"I don't mind," Sara Lynn said as she retrieved the vacuum and had the hall runner clean in no time. "Now, that's better, isn't it?" she said as she surveyed the results.

"Absolutely," Lillian said.

Sara Lynn said, "I just wanted to come out and wish you two a good night. Lillian, thank you for having us."

"You can stay as long as you'd like," she said. "You know that, don't you?"

"That reminds me. Jennifer, did you tell her the news?"

"What news is that?" I asked, hoping Sara Lynn wasn't going to bring up my living arrangements. I didn't want to fight that particular battle, especially not this late.

"Jennifer's being evicted," Sara Lynn said, and I saw Lillian's face cloud up.

"What are you talking about?"

There was no escaping it now. I brought her up-to-date, and before I could stop her, she was reaching for her telephone. "Don't, Lillian, I can handle this."

"I got you hooked up with Hester Taylor, and I'm not about to let her throw you out on the street like this."

There was no arguing with Lillian, so I kept my thoughts to myself as she punched in her friend's telephone number. After a minute she hung up without saying a word. "I got her machine. Can you believe it? She's already gone, spouting some nonsense about moving to the Florida Keys."

"I think the Keys are beautiful," I said.

"I know how pretty they are, but I didn't think Hester would actually go through with her crazy idea."

"You knew about this?" I asked.

"I just assumed she was daydreaming out loud. Last year she wanted to move to Alaska. The year before that it was Tuscany."

"So where is Jennifer supposed to go now?" Sara Lynn asked.

Before Lillian could reply, I said, "Jennifer's going to bed. You two don't need to worry about where I'm going to live. I'll find a place on my own." Before either one of them could say another word, I said good night and headed off to my room. If I wasn't there with them, they couldn't persuade me to do something I had no intention of doing. I crept silently into the pink bedroom, and from the light shining in from the hallway, I could see Oggie and Nash curled up on my pillows, one cat per pillow. It appeared that they'd had no trouble making themselves at home, but I hoped they didn't get too comfortable.

There was no way I was moving in with Lillian for more than one night.

THEMED CARDS

Want to send a special card that people will cherish long after they receive it? Creating a unique card is as easy as going through your photo album. Find a picture that stirs memories for you and the card's recipient. It can be a photograph taken at summer camp, a birthday party or even a picnic. Make a photocopy of the picture, cut it to the size you'd like, then glue it onto card stock. It makes a wonderful backdrop for whatever message you choose to convey.

Chapter 4

The next morning, I had to rush to get the cats back to my apartment before work. Lillian had gotten up early and had outdone herself with a feast of breakfast for the three of us, and I'm afraid we all dawdled over coffee long past when we should have been getting ready for the day ahead. I'd offered to help clean up, but Lillian had refused my aid on the pretext that I had enough to do as it was. I suspected she'd witnessed a couple of near drops last night when I'd been rinsing her crystal and china, and didn't want to take any chances this morning. Sara Lynn's spirits seemed to be good, so I headed home to get ready for a new day of card making.

At the card shop, I found a message on my machine. I was just starting to play it when the telephone rang.

"Custom Card Creations," I said.

"You've really got the hang of that greeting," Gail, my best friend in the world, said.

"What are you doing up this early? I didn't think you salespeople rolled out of bed until noon."

"Don't kid yourself. The guys I start selling to are up at five a.m., and they expect me to keep their bizarre working hours, if you can imagine that." Gail sold heavy-construction equipment, and if her expensive wardrobe and fancy jewelry were any indication, she was very good at what she did.

"So what's up?" I asked as I sorted through the mail.

"I just wanted to be sure you're still coming to dinner. I heard about what happened last night, but I don't want that to interfere with our plans."

"Why would it?" I asked. "I'm not involved in the murder or the investigation."

I had to hold the telephone away from my ear as she erupted in laughter. After she calmed herself, I asked, "Are you through cackling yet?"

"Sorry, I couldn't help myself. Jennifer Shane, I know there is no way in the world you're not going to poke your nose into Eliza Glade's murder, and I'm not silly enough to ask you not to. But I don't want you to bail on dinner tonight, no matter what the excuse. Reggie said his friend is really excited about meeting you."

"That alone is enough to make me worry," I said.

"Why's that? You're a charming, beautiful woman who owns a successful small business."

I laughed. "Okay, first, thanks for the pep talk, and second, I can't imagine anyone in their right mind being excited about a blind date."

"Don't think of it that way," Gail said. "Consider it an opportunity to meet someone new and interesting."

"In front of you, your new boyfriend, his mother and her date. You're right, no pressure there to be on my best behavior."

Gail laughed again. It was one of the things I loved about her: she had an infectious sense of humor that could win over the coldest heart. "You'll be fine. I promise. Remember, you need to be there by seven. Are you sure you don't want us to pick you up? It's no problem, really."

"I can drive myself, thank you very much. Besides, if I need an excuse to take off, I don't want to have to wait for a ride."

"Ever the skeptic, aren't you? See you tonight," Gail said, then hung up.

Honestly, she was the best friend I could ask for, but she worried about me too much. Whenever she was in love, which was often enough, Gail wanted nothing more than the world to be in love all around her. That meant that over the years I'd had more than my fair share of blind dates and fix-ups, all done to keep my best friend mollified more than in hopes of finding the love of my life. Sometimes I wondered if I'd already found my special someone, and we'd blown it. Greg Langston had looked pretty cozy with his latest love the night before. So where did that leave me? Still looking, I supposed.

The chime over the front door rang, and I looked up expecting to see Lillian. Instead, it was an actual customer—a welcome distraction indeed. A thin young woman with curly blond hair came in and started to look around.

"Is there anything I can help you with?"

"No thanks," she said as she picked up a card, read it, then put it back in the rack.

I watched her do that for ten minutes, then said, "If you can't find exactly what you want, I'm sure I could help you make the perfect card yourself."

The girl said softly, "No, that's way too much trouble."

"For you or for me?" I asked. "Because if you're worried about my time, I'd like nothing better than to help you make something special. After all, that's why I opened the shop."

She looked at me with uncertainty. "Really? You'd really help me make my own card?"

"Absolutely," I said as I joined her and held out my hand. "By the way, I'm Jennifer."

"I'm Krystal," she said.

"It's nice to meet you, Krystal. Now, exactly what kind of card are you looking for?"

"I'd like a get-well card for my mom. She's in the hospital."

"Okay," I said as I led her to our supplies. "First off, what's your mother's favorite color?"

"She's a nut for anything blue," the girl admitted.

I led her to the card stock and fancy papers we carried. "Pick out a shade you think she'd like."

She did as I asked, opting for a midnight blue. I grabbed a sheet of lighter blue, and a few other sheets, too. "We'll use these as complementary colors. Now what's her favorite thing in the world?"

Krystal didn't even have to think about it. "She loves her flower garden passionately."

"Perfect," I said, and led her to the selection of pressed, dried flowers we had. "Would you like to choose some, or should I?"

"I like these," she said as she selected a small, flat bouquet of blue flowers. I took them from her, grabbed a sheet of rub-on letters and a few scraps of paper, and led her to our worktable by the window.

"Let's see, I know I've got just the right punch here somewhere." I searched through the box of large paper punches, and found the one I wanted. I punched out a vase shape from the dark blue paper, then laid Krystal's flowers on a sheet of the lighter blue stock. "Just put the vase over the stems and see what you think."

She did as I asked, then said, "It's beautiful."

"And easy, too," I said. "We have sheets of scripted sentiments made up if you'd like to just say 'Get Well,' but if you'd like to personalize your card more, you can use these letters. You just rub the letter you want onto the paper with this burnisher and you're all set."

She took the stylus from me and said, "It's just a chunk of wood."

"Actually, it's a carefully sculpted piece of hard maple with a polyurethane finish, but you can call it a chunk if you want to."

She studied the layout of her card, then asked, "Should I glue all this down before I do the lettering?"

"The best way to approach it is to figure out where you want everything to go first, then letter on the flat paper before you start assembling your card."

She rubbed a message to her mother on the paper, then I helped her arrange the vase and flowers with doubled-sided tape. Then we matted three different pieces of paper together, one just a little bigger than the next, to form a perfect border. After that, we attached the front to another piece of folded card stock and we were finished.

"Now pick out an envelope, and we're set."

She chose a blue one—surprise, surprise—and I rang up her purchase. Krystal looked puzzled when she saw the amount. "Is there something wrong?" I asked.

"You charged me the same as one of your regular cards," she said. "It should be more."

"I'd say you could leave me a tip, but as the store owner I'd just have to turn it down. Krystal, why on earth should I charge you more for something I had fun helping with?"

"I don't know," she said. "It just doesn't seem right."

"If you'd like, I could always overcharge you next time you come in," I said with a smile.

"No thanks, that's all right, but I'll be back. That was fun."

"I'm glad you enjoyed yourself."

After she was gone, I started to clean up our mess, then I remembered that I needed to make a card for Addie Mason at Heaven Scent. I'd liked the way Krystal's card had turned out, so I decided to make a bouquet myself. Not blue though, I'd had my fill of that. I chose a nice pink and white collection of pressed flowers, then chose a patterned pink-and-white paper for my cutout vase. After some experimenting, I was happy with the results and set everything in place with doubled-sided tape. I didn't care about a personalized message on the front, so I chose one that said, "With My Deepest Sympathy" and affixed the sticker to the card. It was quite lovely, actually, and I decided that as soon as Lillian came in, I'd make a few for my shelves. I generated a fair profit selling my cards, but the real joy came from the creative process.

Lillian walked in as I was finishing the card, and said, "It's too pink."

"What can I say? I was inspired by your guest bedroom last night."

She shook her head. "Then I'm going to repaint this weekend. It always was a little too feminine for my taste."

"I think it's really very nice," I said. "I made this for Addie. Should I do another one instead?"

Lillian shook her head. "It's perfect for her." She glanced at her watch. "Is it too early to go over there now?"

"Lillian, what makes you think she'll even open the shop today? After all, her business partner just died last night."

My aunt said, "If you knew Addie as well as I did, you'd realize she'd never pass up the chance to make a dollar or two, no matter who died. Remember,

Heaven Scent is her life. Besides, where else is she going to go? But there's one factor that overrides everything else, that makes me positive we'll find her at the shop this morning."

"What's that?"

"I went by there on my way here and saw that she was open for business. Are you ready to go?"

"I'd like to make a little money first before we shut the place down," I said.

"I suppose," she said. "What would you like me to do this morning?"

"You could make more pink cards," I said, just to see the look of disdain on my aunt's face. "Or you could watch the shop while I make them."

"That one, I choose that one," she said with enthusiasm.

I was working on a card when Bradford came in, a look of distress replacing his usual smile.

"What's wrong?" I asked him.

"Sara Lynn just blew me off," he said. "I can cut her a little slack, but if she keeps this up, I'm going to have to take her in on general principle."

Lillian said, "She's had quite a shock, what with Bailey walking out on her and all."

"So you knew about the affair, too."

"Come on, Bradford," I said. "We're family. She told us last night."

He shook his head. "I've known about it for a few weeks. I hated to tell her about it, but she had a right to know. Now she'll barely speak to me."

To our surprise, Lillian patted Bradford's arm lightly. "Shooting the messenger has been a well-respected reaction to bad news throughout the course of time. You did the right thing telling her."

"Thanks. That's something, I guess."

Before Lillian could retort and end the pleasantries between them, I asked, "Is she really a suspect in the murder?"

"Jen, I wish I could say she wasn't, but I'd be lying. The whole town knows how much she and Eliza hated each other, and that was before Bailey started sleeping with Eliza. She had an argument in the kitchen last night not two feet from where we found the body half an hour later. You do the math. I'm getting heat from the mayor's office, and he's threatening to call the governor if I don't arrest our big sister."

"Can he do that?" I asked.

Bradford shook his head. "I doubt the governor of Virginia has time to take his call, but you never know. I've been trying to eliminate Sara Lynn as a suspect all morning, but every time I find something, it looks even worse for her than it did before. She won't answer my questions, and I can't help her if she won't talk to me."

"Would you like me to talk to her?" I asked. "She might tell me something she's holding back from you."

Bradford slammed his palm down on my worktable. "She's got to get it through her head that I'm trying to help her. I swear, she's more stubborn than you and Lillian put together."

"I doubt that," Lillian said. "Let us talk to her, Bradford. You can come along if you'd like."

"No thanks," he said, shaking his head firmly. "I'm going back over there and I'm not leaving until I get some answers from her. Thanks for the pep talk, though."

Grady Farrar, owner of Farrar Hardware and now interim president of the Rebel Forge chamber of commerce, came into the shop as Bradford was leaving. He was holding a paper bag in his hand as if it contained something valuable.

"Did I miss something?" Grady asked.

"Nothing that matters," I said. "What brings you here, Grady? Are you looking for a card for that lovely wife of yours?"

"Jennifer, if I brought a card home to Martha, she'd think I was up to something. No thank you, trouble like that I don't need."

Lillian said, "So if you're not here for a card, to what do we owe the pleasure of your company?"

He held the paper bag out to me. "I forgot all about this in the excitement last night. Here, this belongs to you."

I took the bag and opened it. Inside was the golden anvil I'd won last night just as Eliza's body had been discovered.

I tried to hand it back to him as I said, "I can't take it."

"Now, Jennifer, don't make me scold you in public. You won it fair and square; it belongs to you. About that speech I made last night," he added softly, "those were Eliza's words, not mine. I'd never have read them if I'd realized how hurtful they were going to be. She had no right to go after your sister like that." Grady looked flustered. "And here I am speaking ill of the dead. It was a long night and a short sleep for me, but that's no excuse. If you ladies will pardon me, I'll be heading back to my hardware store."

After he was gone, I put the paper bag on the counter. Lillian asked, "Aren't you even going to take it out of the bag? Let me see it, Jennifer. I'm curious about it, even if you're not."

"They never should have given it to me in the first place," I said. "And I have a sneaking suspicion they wouldn't have if Eliza hadn't seen it as a way to take a jab at Sara Lynn."

Lillian ignored me and took the anvil out of the

bag. "Nonsense, it's your award. Where should we put it?"

"How about back in the bag?" I suggested.

"It needs to be displayed," Lillian said, ignoring me completely. "I know. Let's have a shelf installed for it above the register. That way everyone will know you won it."

"Lillian, let me have that."

She reluctantly handed the anvil to me, and I put it in the display counter under the cash register.

"Jennifer, you can hardly see it there."

"Lillian, if I catch you moving it, you're fired, and I mean it."

My aunt took in my stern stare, then said somberly, "We can't have that, can we? I don't know how I'd manage to squeak by without my salary from the shop."

After a second, we both burst out laughing. Lillian could buy and sell my shop a dozen times over, and we both knew it. Besides, she didn't draw a dime in pay, if I didn't include the supplies she freely used.

"So when are we going to Heaven Scent?" Lillian asked. "I'm going crazy just hanging around here."

"Okay, you wore me down. Let me hang the sign on the door and we'll go." I'd invested in a sign that offered the adjustable hands of a clock and set it for an hour's time. It would be enough time to talk to Addie, and hopefully I wouldn't lose too many customers while we were gone. Business had really picked up since I'd first opened the card shop, but I knew that I could fail at any moment if I ignored the clientele I'd fought so hard to build. Summer was coming, and with it an influx of tourists who would hopefully keep me in the black for the year, and I knew I wouldn't be able to leave the shop as easily as I could now. That was how I justified my sketchy hours from time to time, knowing how busy I was going to be very soon. If Sara Lynn's shop Forever Memories was any indication, I'd probably have to hire a few part-time college kids to help me keep up. I knew just who I'd like to hire, too. I'd babysat for Corrine Knotts a long time ago, and she'd grown into a very capable and friendly young woman now in college. I'd have to ask her mother for her phone number so I could hire Corrine before somebody else nabbed her. It was just one more item for my to-do list.

"Honestly, Jennifer, let's go."

"I've never seen you this eager to go anywhere in your life," I said as I put the sign up on the door.

"I'm worried if we don't do something soon, your brother's not going to have any choice. If he has to arrest Sara Lynn, I doubt she'll ever speak to him again. We all have our differences from time to time, but we're all the family we've got, and I won't see our bonds destroyed."

"Hang on a second," I said when we were outside. "I forgot something."

"Jennifer, is it absolutely necessary?"

I grinned at her. "It's going to be hard to give her a sympathy card if we don't take it with us."

I grabbed the card, and then dead-bolted the shop door. Heaven Scent was just down the block, so at least we didn't have far to walk. It was a good thing, too, because as we made our way down Oakmont, it started to rain. Though the day had been warm enough, the raindrops were chilled and stung as they hit. We made it to Heaven Scent just in time. As Lillian and I rushed into the store, the sky opened up and we were in the middle of a full-scale rainstorm.

"Where did that come from?" Lillian asked me as we caught our breath.

"I'm not sure," I said as I looked around the shop.

I'd been in Heaven Scent a few times in the past, but the mixes of aromas were stronger than I'd remembered. The shelves were lined with bath soaps, fragrances, candles and batches of potpourri. If it contained a scent and a tourist might want it, Heaven Scent was bound to carry it. There were also wind chimes and dream catchers hanging in the window, along with a vast selection of stained-glass trinkets that must have caught the sunlight and spread it around the room. If there'd been any sunlight, anyway. Eliza also ran an accounting service on the side from the back room of the store. She'd approached me about keeping my books when I'd first opened, but I could keep track of my corporate assets with a checkbook and a calculator. At the time, Eliza had told me that she ran the small operation mostly just to keep her hand in her former profession, but scents and aromas were her first and true love.

There were no customers in the shop when we walked in, and I was beginning to wonder if Addie was there herself. "Hello?" I called out, hoping to get someone's attention.

"One second," I heard someone shout from the back room. Hanging out in the empty store, I was suddenly glad for every customer I'd ever had. I knew business would pick up for all of us once the summer started, but how in the world did anybody survive the other nine months of the year?

Addie Mason came out of the back room, brushing some of her frizzy red hair out of her face as she put a folder bulging with papers on the counter. Her eyes were red, and I wondered why she'd come to work so soon after losing her business partner. She looked even thinner than normal to me in her emerald green pantsuit, and I pondered, not for the first time, exactly how much she weighed. Actually, I didn't want to know. It would probably just depress me.

Addie looked surprised when she saw that Lillian and I were her customers. She said curtly, "Don't tell me you're out in this mess shopping."

I held my card out to her. "We just wanted to come by and tell you how sorry we are about Eliza."

She took the card, but didn't open it. "I should probably thank you for the thought," Addie said, "but to be honest with you, I'm kind of surprised to see you both here."

"Why? Can't we visit you to express our sympathy?" Lillian asked.

Addie frowned. "Don't pretend we all don't know who did it. Sara Lynn didn't try that hard to hide it."

"My sister didn't kill your partner," I said.

Addie didn't answer, but her eye roll was enough for me.

"Come on, you know Sara Lynn isn't capable of doing that."

She said, "You're wrong. There's no doubt in my mind that she did it."

The blunt callousness of her words shocked me. Without thinking, I said, "What makes you think the police aren't looking at you as a suspect?"

Lillian touched my arm. "Jennifer, that's enough."

I pulled away. "She started it. Sara Lynn didn't kill Eliza."

Addie nearly shouted, "You're her sister, I understand why you'd take up for her, but I'm not about to let anybody pin it on me. I'm innocent." There was real anger in Addie's eyes as she stared at me.

"So you say." I gestured around the room. "Who gets her share of the business now? Does it all go to you?"

Addie blushed—an easy giveaway, considering her pale skin. "So what if it does? That doesn't mean I killed her. Your sister had a lot more reason to want Eliza dead than I did. Since it's pretty obvious you didn't come here to buy anything, I'm going to have to ask you to leave."

"I wouldn't dream of staying somewhere I wasn't welcome," I said.

I'd started for the door when she called out, "You forgot something."

She held the card out to me, but I wouldn't take it. "Whether you believe it or not, the sentiment in there is real," I said.

"I don't need your sympathy," Addie said. Then she tore the card I'd worked so hard on in half, and dropped both pieces on the floor. I started toward her, but I couldn't break through Lillian's restraining grip.

"Come on, Jennifer. Let's go."

My aunt practically dragged me out of the shop onto the sidewalk. The rain had lessened some, but it was still coming down at a good clip.

"Where do we go now?" I asked.

"Back to the card shop," Lillian said as she stormed off, and I had little choice but to follow her.

We got back to Custom Card Creations and I unlocked the door. By the time we got inside, the rain had practically stopped. Lillian grabbed a few towels from the back and threw one to me.

"That went well, wouldn't you say?" Her voice was dripping with sarcasm.

"She started it," I said.

"What are you, in third grade? We went there to get information, not start a common brawl."

"We found out what we wanted to know," I said. "She practically admitted that she would inherit Eliza's share of the shop. What else do we need to know?"

Lillian thought about it a moment, then said, "Let's see, I wanted to ask her if she had an alibi for last night, if she knew anyone else who might want her partner dead, if Eliza had any family she was close to, who was handling the estate . . . little things like that. Jennifer, if you're going to keep looking into this, you're going to have to learn to control your temper."

"I'm sorry," I muttered, hating every second that Lillian was right. I'd lost it when that woman had accused my sister of murder, and by blowing up, I'd cut us off from a possible source of information.

"I can fix this," I said softly.

"I don't see how. Give me a second to think this through." Lillian paced around the shop as I dried my hair with the towel. It would be frizzier than I liked, but I didn't have time to mess with it at the moment. I was just glad I'd already planned to go back to my apartment before dinner tonight.

"I've got an idea," Lillian finally said.

"Tell me. I'll do whatever it takes."

She shook her head. "I don't think so. If I bring you in there right now, it will be like throwing gasoline on a bonfire. But if I manage to get seven words in, I think I can smooth things over with her."

"I can't imagine what those seven words could possibly be," I said.

"Just let me worry about that," Lillian said. "This might take some time."

"Take all you need," I said, regretting again the way I'd blown up. After Lillian was gone on her mission of reconciliation, I tried to put myself in Addie's place. Not only had she lost a business partner, but she and Eliza had been close on a personal level. And what did I do? I waltzed in there like I'd owned the place, and started in on her. Not good, Jennifer. Not good at all.

I tried to distract myself with card making, but for one of the few times in my life, I just wasn't in the mood. A customer or two would have been great, but, just my luck, the brief rainstorm earlier had evidently kept the shoppers at home. When the chime finally announced a visitor, I was willing to give away half the store to keep them there.

Then I saw that it was Greg Langston, probably the only person on earth I didn't want to see at the moment.

Chapter 5

"Does your girlfriend know you're here?" I asked, immediately regretting my harsh choice of words. Somehow Greg brought the worst out in me lately, and I couldn't seem to stop myself from firing verbal shots at him. All in all, I was not having a good day dealing with people, and I wondered if I should just go home—while I still had one—lock my door, take my phone off the hook, and pull the covers over my head until this attitude of mine passed.

Greg let my snippy question slide. "Stephanie would have a fit, but this isn't about her, it's about you. What's going on?"

"I don't know what you're talking about," I said as innocently as I could manage.

"Come on, I saw the way you stormed past my shop earlier. You weren't out on a social call."

I looked at the clock. "Greg, that was almost half an hour ago. What took you so long, if you were worried about me?"

He suddenly got the guiltiest look on his face, and I knew why he hadn't come over.

"What's the matter, were you too busy giving her private lessons? Don't tell me, your new girlfriend suddenly developed a strong interest in pottery. Or is it just the potter?" Even as I said it, I wondered where that had come from.

"Jennifer, do you honestly think you have the right to ask me that? You're the one who didn't want me any more, remember? You can't act jealous now if I happen to be seeing someone else."

It didn't help my temper knowing that he was right. "You know what? That's absolutely true. In answer to your question, I'm fine," I said. "Thanks for stopping by."

"You're not going to brush me off that easily," Greg said. "Just because we're not together doesn't mean I don't still care about you."

"Do it from your shop then, would you? I've got cards to make." I walked to the door and held it open for him. After a few seconds, he took the hint and left, but not before saying, "Be careful, Jen. You have a tendency to get into things too deep before you realize what you're doing."

"Thanks for the advice," I said. I wanted him out of there before I said anything else I'd come to regret later.

He shook his head, then walked away.

I cried out in frustration once he was gone as I swept a box full of custom-made paper off the counter. Just my luck, the seal came loose in midflight, and an avalanche of paper wafted down to the floor. Why did I let him get to me like that?

Lillian walked in as I was trying to collect the errant papers. "I'm sorry I missed the parade. It must have really been something if that's the size of the confetti. Do you want to tell me what happened?"

"No, I can't afford to have you disappointed in me twice in one day. I had a little tantrum, but I'm all better now. What did Addie say?"

"Well, it took some time and a little feather stroking, but I finally convinced her that we meant well with our visit. In fact, she wanted me to tell you that she was sorry she destroyed your beautiful card. I helped her piece it back together, and she really was touched."

I shook my head. "I don't know how you do it, but I'm hoping you're willing to teach me. I thought it was hopeless when you said you were going back in there."

Lillian squatted down and helped me gather the rest of the paper. "You actually might have helped more than you realize. I had the distinct impression Addie needed to blow off some steam before she came apart, and you just happened to be handy."

"Hey, what can I say? Everybody needs a special purpose in life. So what's your gut reaction? Did she do it?"

Lillian paused a moment, then said, "She could have. When I asked her about her alibi, there were at least ten minutes she couldn't account for. She claims she ducked out of Hurley's to get her inhaler from Heaven Scent, but nobody saw her go, or, more importantly, come back. The store's worth quite a bit, despite their low sales at the moment. The two of them owned the building outright, and it all goes to Addie now. The only person left alive with any family connection to Eliza is Luke Penwright, and once they were divorced, she made sure to change her will. Addie said Eliza couldn't wait to disinherit him."

I couldn't believe the flood of information. "How did you manage to get all that out of her in just half an hour?"

"That just took five minutes," Lillian admitted. "Your little tirade loosened her up, and by the time I walked in, she was dying to tell someone how wrong you were."

"So what do we do now?"

Lillian looked at the clock, then said, "I'm going to take a long lunch, and when I get back an hour before closing, I'm going to take over so you can go to your apartment and get ready for your date tonight."

"It's not a date," I said automatically. "I was talking about the case."

Lillian shrugged. "I've got a few calls to make, but they can wait. Jennifer, you can't let this ruin your evening. If nothing else, I don't think Gail would ever forgive you."

"I still think we should keep digging," I said. "Proving that Sara Lynn is innocent is more important than my social life this evening."

"That's where you're wrong," Lillian said. "You don't get out nearly enough, and I won't let you cancel this. We can investigate more tomorrow, I promise, but just for tonight, I want you to concentrate on having fun. Okay?"

"Okay," I agreed reluctantly.

Lillian nodded. "Then I'm off."

She was gone again before I could stop her. I hadn't eaten yet, either, and I didn't want to wait until four o'clock to have my lunch. I should have known she'd realize that, though. Thirty minutes later, a waiter named Tommy from Hurley's showed up with a hamburger and fries. As I offered to pay him, he said, "It's taken care of, and the tip, too. I don't know how you managed it, but I didn't even think we delivered our food."

"I'm special," I said as I slipped him a five despite his instructions. Tommy was in college—I'd heard Jack saying something about it the night before—and while he put up a token protest about taking more money, I managed to convince him just the same.

I felt worlds better after I'd eaten, but the threatening skies kept things quiet in the shop, and I couldn't bring myself to make any more cards. I finally just gave up and grabbed the paperback mystery I'd been reading during my spare moments, from where it was stored safely away in my purse.

Dame Agatha Christie herself couldn't hold my attention as I kept thinking about Eliza Glade's killer. Someone had to have had the guts of a second-story man to kill her with all those potential witnesses just on the other side of the door. Had the perpetrator planned to kill her with the letter opener from the start, or had it been a weapon of opportunity once the murderer was on-site? I knew Bradford thought that anybody could be a killer given the right circumstances. I couldn't imagine being able to bring myself to do it, and I hoped I never would.

The next few hours felt like an eternity until Lillian finally showed up again.

"How was lunch?" she asked as she took off her coat.

"It was great. Let me pay you for it," I said as I reached for my purse.

"Please, it was the least I could do," she said. "Have you had many customers since I left?"

"For all the good I did, I might as well have gone home right after you left."

"Don't worry, Jennifer, soon enough we'll be longing for the good old quiet days."

"I hope you're right," I said as I straightened the counter displays for the fourth time in two hours. "If you'd like, why don't we just shut the shop down an hour early and you can go home, too."

Lillian shook her head. "I don't mind working until five," she said.

"Really, I'm fine with it. In fact, I'd feel better if you took off, too."

"That's nonsense. I have nothing else I need to do."

Something was going on. Normally my aunt would jump at the chance to go home early, even though she was only a volunteer and could come and go as she wished. "What is it? What aren't you telling me? You're not having a man meet you here, are you?"

"Jennifer Shane, I have enough places to entertain my gentleman friends without using your store as a rendezvous point."

"Then what is it? I'm not going until you tell me."

She frowned, then finally said, "If you must know, I've made a few telephone calls, and I'm hoping I get some answers before we close."

"Is there anything I should know about?" I asked.

"I won't know that until I get my answers," Lillian said plainly.

I held her hands in mine. "You didn't do anything silly, did you? I won't have you taking unnecessary risks, Lillian."

"You worry too much," she said as she withdrew her hands. "Now go. Have a lovely evening."

"Be careful," I said as she ushered me out of the door of my own shop.

"I'd say the same thing to you, but it might just do you some good to take a chance tonight. I expect a full report in the morning, Jennifer."

"You're overly optimistic about a blind date," I said.

"I thought you said it wasn't anything like that."

I was outside by that point. "So I lied. I'll see you tomorrow."

Oggie and Nash were waiting by my door when I walked into my apartment. They both looked too smug for my taste, so I looked around, and sure enough, someone had been foolish enough to slide a note to me under my door. Short of a roomful of catnip, there was nothing my cats loved more than shredding paper. I found remnants spread throughout the apartment, and to their credit, my roommates had been terribly efficient. There wasn't even enough of it left to read the handwriting, a monumental feat given the required level of destruction.

"So who came by?" I asked. "Did you happen to see enough of the handwriting to tell who it was from before you shredded it?"

They both stared at me as if they were fascinated by my discourse, but I knew better. Most likely they were waiting for dinner. Of course, they were waiting for dinner at most times of the day or night.

"What am I going to do with you two?" I asked as I knelt down to stroke Nash's coat. Oggie, normally not one to seek out attention, joined us, weaving in and out between my legs. After a few minutes, he grew tired of the maneuver and plopped himself down in front of the cabinet where I kept the cat food. Nash would have allowed me to spoil him all night if I'd been so inclined, but I only had so much time, and I had to shampoo my hair as well. After I fed them, I took a quick shower and was ready a good five minutes before it was time to leave. I'd changed into my nicest dress for the occasion, a burgundy number that made me look sleek and graceful, as hard as that was for most of the people who knew me to believe. I'd given up eating lunch out for a month to afford it, but it had been worth every missed bite. When I wore it, I felt good. What more could I ask from a dress?

One of my downstairs neighbors was just coming in as I walked out the door. Barrett was a handsome man about my age, but he had a problem with an ex-girlfriend that I found irritating. Namely, he refused to let her go, and she constantly kept popping in and out of his life at the most inopportune times.

His eyes widened when he saw me, and I swear I could hear him suck in some air. "Jennifer, you look lovely this evening."

"Thanks," I said. "I've got a date." Hey, a blind date counted, didn't it?

"I'm not surprised. Have you found a new place to live yet?"

"I just got the note yesterday," I said. "We've got a week, don't we?"

He shook his head. "You must not have read the latest from our ungracious landlady. We now have three days to move, if we expect to get our security deposits back. She's so eager to evict us, she even offered to return last month's rent as a bonus. It seems she's got a rather eager buyer lined up ready to take possession of the property."

"Can she do that?" I asked. "Surely we've got to have some recourse. What does Jeffrey say?"

"Our friend has already left the premises," Barrett said. "I'm surprised he didn't say good-bye."

"I got a note from someone," I admitted. "I'm just not sure who it was."

He looked at me quizzically, and I almost left him in suspense, but I didn't want anyone in Rebel Forge to think I was any crazier than I actually was. "My cats shredded it. They do that."

He nodded sympathetically, and I found myself drawn to him again, even though I knew he was bad for me. I'd have to be a little kinder to Oggie and Nash. There were more kinds of catnip than the one they were addicted to. "So where will you go?" he asked.

"I'll land on my feet," I said. "How about you?"

He didn't want to tell me—I could see it in his eyes—but he finally admitted, "Penny's asked me to move back in with her, and we've decided to give it another try."

Penny was the aforementioned girlfriend who would never quite go away. "I wish you both the best of luck," I said, then I got out of there before I told him how I really felt.

As I drove the Gremlin toward the outskirts of town to the house where I was meeting Gail and her boyfriend, I found myself wondering what attracted me to certain men and not others. For the life of me, I couldn't find a yardstick or a general rule that explained my attractions in the past. Maybe I was better off not knowing. That way I'd always be surprised.

When Gail had told me her boyfriend lived in a large house, I'd expected a two-story Victorian with a large front porch. Instead, I found a gated entrance off the road, and followed a winding path through a small field of grass before I saw a mansion that must have been a hundred years old. The gray stone structure was massive, almost the size of a castle. I couldn't imagine paying the heating bill for it, let alone what the property taxes must have amounted to.

I parked the Gremlin in the looping front driveway, not sure if I wanted to get out or not. I looked as silly parked there as an elephant in tap shoes. But what could I tell Gail—that the structure itself intimidated me? I was still debating what to do when the massive, weathered oak door in front swung open and Gail herself stepped out.

Despite my earlier misgivings, I got out of the Gremlin as Gail approached. She was wearing an emerald green cocktail dress that looked elegant and classy. Gail's auburn hair had been expertly styled, and she looked exactly like royalty should look. We weighed nearly the same, though I was a good six inches taller than she was, but somehow Gail managed to convey the image that she was the perfect size, while I always felt like I could stand to lose a pound or twenty.

"Wow, you clean up pretty good," I said.

"Look who's talking. I'm going to have to be diligent tonight or you're going to steal my boyfriend without even meaning to."

"Let's just admit that we both look fabulous, and move on," I said. "Are you sure about this?"

"Positive," she said as she locked an arm in mine. Was it that obvious I'd just been considering flight? "Let's go. Reggie and his mother are waiting for us."

When we walked in, I was astounded to see a huge formal entryway, complete with a chandelier and an Oriental carpet. "This is one heck of a first impression."

Gail smiled. "Mostly we go in and out through the side door, but I wanted you to get the full effect tonight."

"It's really something," I said.

"We're right through here," Gail said as she led the way. I wasn't sure what Reggie Bloom's family had done to be able to afford such an expensive place, but I was willing to bet it had been done generations ago. As we entered what was surely the formal dining room, I saw a man about my age talking with a classic-looking older woman. The man—who had to be Reggie—was sandy haired and had the build of a football player. Did I know him? Our area wasn't that big, so I didn't doubt I'd seen him around, but something else nagged at my mind. I'd seen him, and recently, too. I wouldn't have said he was handsome until he turned toward us and smiled. It was amazing how it transformed his face. Before that, he'd been brooding, as if he and his mother were repeating an argument they'd had many times before. The mother, a striking, petite woman in her mid-fifties, showed where Reggie had inherited his smile as she greeted me.

As she took my hand, she said, "You must be Jennifer. You look absolutely lovely tonight."

"So do you, Mrs. Bloom," I said. It was true, too. She was dressed in a simple gray outfit that was no doubt worth more than four or five of my cars, and that didn't even begin to approach her shoes or the diamonds she wore as embellishments.

"Please, call me Helena," she said. "I'm afraid my father had delusions of grandeur when it came to naming his children. If you can believe it, he actually wanted to call my younger brother Zeus, but my mother put her foot down."

"So what did they finally settle on?"

"Troy, if you can imagine it. We all called him T, though, by his wish, as soon as he learned to talk. I miss his laugh."

"I'm so sorry," I said, not sure what else to say.

"He led a good life, one he enjoyed to the utmost— a lesson we would all do well to follow," Helena said. She grasped my hands tightly as she added, "Jennifer, I'm afraid I've got some bad news."

"I'll tell her, Mother," Reggie said. "After all, it's my responsibility."

"Yes, but it's my home. Jennifer, I'm afraid your date had to cancel at the last second. Something about an unexpected business trip," she added as she raised one eyebrow at her son. "I wish I had a camera, so I could take a picture and show the young fool just what he missed tonight."

"Thanks for the sentiment," I said as I started for the door. "If you all don't mind, I'd just as soon not be a fifth wheel tonight."

"Now where on earth do you think you're going?" Helena asked me. "Just because Claude can't make it, that's no reason we should be deprived of your company."

As a single woman in her thirties, I'd been in enough situations where I was the odd person out, and it never got any easier. Even with Helena and Gail urging me to stay, I still felt uneasy about it, but then I decided to have dinner with them after all. How many times was I willing to dress that fancy for an evening meal, anyway?

When I agreed, Helena said, "Let me call Martin and we can begin."

"Is Martin your husband?" I asked innocently enough.

Before Helena could answer, Reggie said, "No, he's just a friend of the family. My father's sick, so he won't be joining us."

"We're among friends," Helena said. "You can tell the truth. I'm afraid it's a bit more serious than that. Peter is dying. He has been for the last ten years, the poor dear, but he wants this house filled with food, friends and laughter, and I mean to abide by my husband's wishes."

What had Gail gotten me into? I looked over at her, and I could see that she was as uncomfortable as I was with the declaration.

An older man with graying temples soon joined us, and the five of us sat down to dinner. The food was delightful—lobster and filet mignon were among the choices—and I soon forgot that I had actually been stood up.

As we waited for dessert to be served, Martin said, "Did you all hear about the murder in town last night? Tragic event, that."

I wasn't about to admit that I'd been there, and

when I saw that Gail was about to say something, I gave her a short burst of my "shut up" look.

When no one rose to the bait, Martin continued. "I understand a shop woman did it. Seems her husband was stepping out on her with the victim. They were having some tawdry affair. These commoners have no more morality than alley cats."

I tried to keep my mouth shut, honestly I did. So nobody was more surprised than I was when I said, "The woman you're referring to is my sister, and while it's true that Eliza was having an affair with her husband, Sara Lynn did not kill her."

I felt my cheeks burning from the statement, but there was nothing I could do about it now. I was certain that same conversation was going on around dinner tables all over Rebel Forge, but that didn't mean I had to sit and listen to it while I was eating. I stood up and put my napkin on my plate. Reggie looked at me with real venom in his gaze, but Helena's look was pure sympathy. "How dreadful for you," she said as she stood, too. "I think a walk around the grounds would be excellent before we tackle dessert. Coming, Jennifer?"

I wanted to storm out of there in righteous indignation, but my hostess had been so gracious throughout the evening, there was no way I could say no to her.

Reggie and Gail stood as well. "We'll join you, Mother," he said.

Helena waved a hand in their direction. "No, Jennifer and I need some time to get acquainted. You two can stay here." Then she looked at Martin. "You, on the other hand, have my permission to leave."

He protested, "I didn't mean anything by it. I was just making conversation."

Helena didn't say a word. She just stood there staring at him until he finally pushed away from the table.

"I'm afraid I'll have to leave after all. Got a pile of work on my desk, you know. Thanks for the meal, Helena. It was lovely, as usual."

He excused himself, and Helena and I left. My shoes weren't exactly designed for hiking, but they worked perfectly for strolling on the carefully manicured grounds.

"Forgive him, my dear, he's a boor at times, but Martin can be a dear friend."

"You didn't have to throw him out on my account," I said.

"I don't have many joys in my life at the moment. Surely you wouldn't rob me of that?"

I matched her grin. "Well, I wouldn't want to do that."

After a few moments, Helena said, "It's a lovely night, isn't it? I just adore this time of year."

"I do, too," I admitted. As we strolled through the gardens and across the landscaped terraces, I found myself sharing more with Helena than I'd ever intended. Somehow during our walk, the topic shifted to my current living conditions, and I told her that my cats and I had been evicted, and were looking for a new place to stay.

"You have cats? How delightful. I'm afraid Reggie's been allergic since he was a boy, and I had to give up my sweet Elysium. Jennifer, may I come visit you and your roommates, as you so charmingly put it?"

"Absolutely. Don't expect a warm reception, though. Oggie and Nash aren't known for their charms at first glance."

"Nor should they be," Helena said. "That's why I've always admired cats. They are honest about how they feel to the point of brutality." She paused, then said, "Jennifer, come with me. There's something I'd like to show you."

I had no idea where she was leading me, but I soon found myself in front of a charming little cabin nestled in a small grove of trees. She went in ahead of me and flipped on the main light. Warm oak pillars stood tall inside, with pastel shades covering the drywall between them.

"It's a timber frame," I said in delight. "I didn't know they made buildings like this so small. I always thought they were grand, sweeping structures."

"We had a framer and his crew come down from Vermont to build it. It's only five hundred square feet, but there's a kitchen, a modest bathroom, and a loft for sleeping. You're not afraid of heights, are you?"

"No, ma'am. I had the top bunk every time I went to summer camp."

She smiled. "Good. Elysium used to love pouncing on me from up there."

"The way the cabin is situated, no one would ever even know it's here."

"That was my plan," Helena said. "Once upon a time I wanted to be an artist more than anything in the world. I spent many joyous hours here away from the world."

"So why did you stop?" I asked. There was no sign of easel, paint or canvas anywhere.

Helena sighed. "I wish I knew. One morning I woke up, and the joy was gone from it, utterly and completely. A few years later, I had it converted into a guest cottage, though no one's ever stayed here. They all seem to prefer the main house."

"I think they're nuts," I said as I looked around. "This place is perfect."

"I was hoping you'd think so. Jennifer, if you'd like it, it's yours."

It took me a second to realize what she was saying. "Pardon me?"

Helena laughed. "I'm not deeding it to you, but I'd be delighted if you'd stay here. I have only one request."

"Name it," I said. This place was perfect for me, and I knew Oggie and Nash would love it, too. There were ledges throughout the small space, and my cats had natural inclinations to scale to the highest spot in any room—in order to look down on their loyal subjects, no doubt.

"I would like to be able to visit with you and your cats on occasion. Don't worry, I'd never come in without your permission, but it would be a delight having cats on the property again."

"Are you sure Reggie won't mind?" I was thinking of his allergies, but from Helena's reaction, she'd obviously come to a different conclusion.

"No matter what my son may think, I'm still in charge around here. Oh, I suppose I'll have to charge you a nominal amount of rent, but it will be a pittance, I assure you."

"What kind of pittance did you have in mind?" I asked, knowing how bare my budget for housing was.

"What do you think is appropriate? For example, what were you paying for your attic loft?"

I named the figure, and Helena said, "Then let's say half that, shall we? Reggie won't have any right to complain that you're taking advantage of me if I'm charging you rent."

I shook my head. "Not enough, though. Helena, I don't want to cause any bad feelings between you and your son."

She touched my shoulder lightly. "That's very thoughtful of you, Jennifer, but the tension was there long before you arrived. So what do you say? Do we have a deal?"

"We do," I said as I took her offered hand. "It's very kind of you, Helena."

"Don't be silly, I have motives of my own."

Back at the house, we entered through the kitchen, and she retrieved a set of keys from a drawer. "This one's to the cottage, and this is for the front gate if the power should ever go out. It was open tonight in your honor, but we normally keep it closed. The code is 5-12-58."

"Got it. Is that somebody's birthday?"

She shook her head. "No, nothing that mundane. Actually, it's the day I met my husband. His father was transferred here near the end of the academic year, and I was asked to show him around school. I was lost to him forever after that." She roused from her reminiscence, and said, "Let's go get that dessert now, shall we?"

I agreed, and was putting the new keys on my ring when we walked back into the dining room. Gail and Reggie were there, obviously expecting us to come in the other way.

"You were gone quite a while," Reggie said. "We were worried about you."

"You shouldn't have been," Helena said. "I have wonderful news. Jennifer's agreed to stay in the cottage. Isn't that delightful? She's bringing her cats with her, too."

"You know I'm allergic to them," Reggie said. "Why on earth did you agree to this?"

"Because I'm still the one who runs this family. I expect you to be courteous to our guest."

Reggie looked like he'd rather eat gravel, but he nodded glumly. "We waited on dessert. Shall I have Matilda serve?"

Helena nodded, and Reggie pushed a button on the

wall summoning the next course. After we ate, Helena said, "If you'll excuse me, I've got a telephone call to make." She took my hands in hers and said, "Jennifer, I can't wait to have you here with us."

"Thanks again, Helena."

"You're most welcome." She turned to Gail and said, "Good night. Thank you for bringing such a delightful guest with you."

"Mother, may I have a word with you?" Reggie asked her.

"Of course. I always have time for you."

I let myself out, and was getting into the Gremlin when Gail flagged me down. I rolled down my window and asked, "What's up? Am I being summoned back inside?"

"No, but I've been pretty effectively dismissed. Reggie asked me to get a ride back to my place with you. Do you mind?"

"Well, I was going out clubbing, but I guess I could drop you off on my way," I said, laughing. I hadn't had much interest going to bars when I'd been in my twenties, and I certainly wasn't about to pick the habit up in my thirties.

"Nightclubbing or card-clubbing?" she said as she got in the passenger side.

"Neither one," I said. "Actually, I need to go home and start packing. I'm sorry if I caused you any trouble in there. If you'd rather I didn't move into the cottage, I'll call Helena in the morning and tell her I've changed my mind."

"You still need a new place to live, don't you?"

"Yes, but not enough to jeopardize our friendship," I replied. "It's easier to find a new address than it is to come up with a new best friend."

She thought about it for a few seconds, then said, "Jennifer, I couldn't live with myself if you turned that place down on my account. Helena certainly took a shine to you, didn't she? I wish she'd smile at me like that just once."

I laughed. "She likes me because I'm not dating her son. You've got two strikes against you from the start. How did you two meet?"

"Thanks for not saying it, but I know what you're thinking. We're an odd match."

"I wouldn't go that far," I said as I swung back out onto the highway. I was going to have a longer commute to work every day, but with that cottage waiting for me, it was going to be worth it.

"It's okay, I'm not sure I understand it myself. There's just something about him that makes my stomach flutter."

"Then that's all the reason you need," I said.

"I am really sorry about tonight," Gail said. "I can't believe Reggie's friend bailed on you at the last second."

"Are you kidding me? He did me a huge favor. If he'd shown up on schedule, there's no way I would have gotten that grand tour, let alone a new place to stay."

"Actually, it was Martin's comment that led to it all." Gail's voice softened as she added, "Jennifer, I didn't have a chance to call you today, but I'm sorry about the rumors going on around town about Sara Lynn."

"You didn't start any of them, did you?" I asked.

"What? Of course not."

I grinned at her. "Then don't apologize for it. That's just one of the things you have to accept when you live in a small town. People talk, and when there's something as high profile as this, they tend to talk a lot. Don't worry. Lillian and I are trying to find alternate suspects for my brother."

"And what does Bradford say about that?"

I shrugged. "He doesn't know yet, and I'm not planning on telling him until we've got our suspect picked out."

"Just be careful," Gail said as I pulled up in front of her condo. "I'd hate to lose you."

"I'm watching every step I take," I said. "Thanks again for tonight. I know it didn't turn out how we'd planned, but I had a lovely time."

"I'll do better at matchmaking the next time," Gail said. "I promise."

"The only promise I want from you is one that says there won't be a next time. I've officially withdrawn my name from the blind-dating pool."

"You can't give up," Gail said. "I know there's somebody out there for you."

"Well, unless he walks into my card shop, he's going to have a hard time finding me. Good night, Gail."

"Night," she said. I waited until she was safely inside before I drove back to my attic apartment. I'd miss the charming space, but in several ways I was trading up. At Helena's, I'd have lots more room, and the cats would have plenty of vantage points from which to peer down at me. Having to see Reggie occasionally would be a negative, but the fact that he was allergic to cats meant that he wouldn't be popping in on me unexpectedly. As for Helena's promised visits, I just hoped Oggie and Nash would be on their best behavior, or I'd be looking for another place to live soon enough.

Chapter 6

"Okay, guys, we're moving," I told Oggie and Nash when I walked into my apartment.

Oggie yowled at me, and I said, "Hey, I don't want to go, either, but we're being evicted." Just then, the door to the bathroom slammed, though none of the windows were open to create a breeze. "Sorry, Frances, it's not my fault." I didn't know if that would mollify the forgetful poltergeist or not, but if she wanted to haunt someone to protest the move, she was going to have to track down Hester Taylor. After all, it was her fault I was leaving.

Unfortunately, I'd become pretty adept at packing in the past few years, so I had a good idea about how to approach it. After I changed into sweats and an old T-shirt, I made a note to get more boxes at the grocery store. As I started jettisoning unwanted items into a trash bag, there was a knock on my door.

I grabbed my aluminum softball bat before I went to the peephole to see who was visiting me. Though Bradford had arranged for a stainless steel door to be installed, I still never answered without some kind of protection, and the bat had served me well in the past.

It was Lillian. I unbolted the door and stepped aside so she could come in.

She looked at me critically, then said, "Jennifer, if

you greet all of your callers that way, I can see how you might have trouble attracting a young man."

"This is the best repellent I know for the bad ones," I said as I locked the door behind her. "You're out awfully late."

"And unfortunately you're not. What happened to your mystery man?"

"He's going to remain one," I said. "He stood me up."

Lillian frowned. "So now they're rejecting you before you even meet? That certainly cuts down on the stress level, doesn't it?"

"It's not all bad," I said. "I found a new place to live."

"I can't imagine how that came about."

I told her about my new arrangement, but she wasn't as happy for me as I'd hoped. "You should be thrilled, Lillian. My problems are over."

"Or are they? Jennifer, you haven't had much contact with people like the Blooms in your life, have you?"

"Just because they have money doesn't mean they're different," I said.

"Nor does it mean they're better," she replied. "Remember that."

"I didn't care for Reggie Bloom, but I found his mother delightful. She's a cat lover, too."

Lillian shook her head. "And that's all you need to vouch for someone else's character, isn't it?"

"I'll admit it goes a long way," I say. "You should see this place, Lillian. It's a beautiful cottage near the main garden, and it's completely separate from the house. Oggie and Nash are going to love it."

"So you haven't taken a room in their home?" Lillian said, acting a little surprised.

"Are you crazy? No, it's all by itself. There's no way I'd be a roomer somewhere, no matter how nice it was. Have you ever been inside the house? It's incredible."

"No, but I dated Peter Bloom at one time, though his name was Bradbury then."

"What are you talking about, Lillian?"

Lillian frowned. "So you don't know everything about your hosts. Their family tradition is that the head of the household is a Bloom, regardless if it's a man or woman. When he married Helena, one of the things Peter had to agree to was to abandon the name Bradbury forever and take his wife's name."

"How odd," I said.

"In this culture, perhaps, but it's not without precedent in the world. That was just the beginning of the changes he was forced to make."

"Well, I like Helena, and the place is perfect for me," I said.

Lillian shrugged. "I take it you've made up your mind, then. You know you can still come live with me if you'd like."

"Thanks, Lillian—I really do appreciate it, but I think it's better for everyone this way."

She nodded, then clapped her hands together. "Then the least I can do is help you pack. I wish Hester was in town, I'd give her a tongue lashing like she's never had in her life. I still can't believe she'd kick you out into the street like this."

"It's all for the best," I said. "I wasn't all that taken with the other people living here."

"They were both less than satisfactory, weren't they?"

As Lillian helped me sort through some of the things I'd accumulated since moving to Whispering

Oak, I said, "So what brings you by here tonight? I know you've got better things to do than to check up on me and my dates."

"Actually, I have some progress to report on our investigation," Lillian said.

"Don't keep me in the dark," I said. "What did you find out?"

"Nothing concrete as of yet," she said. "But I did make an appointment with Polly Blackburn. I told her I was thinking about putting my house on the market, and she jumped at the chance to talk to me."

"Doesn't she realize they'll have to blast you out of there with dynamite to get you to leave?"

Lillian frowned. "I don't know if that's necessarily true anymore. There are times I envy your lifestyle, Jennifer. You change places more often than I change fabric softener. There must be some real advantages to keeping your roots shallow."

I looked at the mess I was in the middle of. "It's not as positive as you think. I hate packing and un-packing, but it's a part of moving." I looked around the attic apartment. "I've grown quite fond of this place," I said. "I'll miss it."

"How about your cats? Will they miss it too, do you think?"

"As far as Oggie and Nash are concerned, as long as their meals come on time and they have one of my pillows to sleep on, they couldn't be more content." I put a few more books on the pile, then said, "What about Luke Penwright? How are you going to get him to talk to you?"

"Actually, we're having lunch tomorrow at Hur-ley's. I was going to suggest The Lunch Box, but he surprised me by asking me to meet him where his ex-wife was murdered. I find that rather odd, don't you?"

"I think he's crazy," I said.

There was another knock on the door, and I told Lillian to be quiet.

I retrieved my bat from the couch, then asked, "Who is it?"

"Jennifer, it's me. Use your peephole."

I unbolted the door and let my brother in. He nodded to Lillian, then bolted the door behind him. "Good girl. I'm proud of you for watching out for yourself."

"I learned my lesson," I said, remembering the time recently when someone had broken into my place. "I don't answer the door without my softball bat. So what brings you out this late? Cindy's going to have your hide." Bradford's wife liked him at home.

"I'm working. She understands it's about family."

I nodded. "So, have you had any luck clearing Sara Lynn's name?"

"Jennifer, that's why I'm here. Do you have any idea where Bailey is right now?"

I didn't even have to think about it. "No, not a clue. How about you, Lillian?"

My aunt shook her head. "He could be in New York by now, for all I know."

"What makes you think he'd go there?" Bradford asked.

"It was just a figure of speech. I could just as easily have said San Francisco."

"But you didn't," Bradford pushed. "You said New York."

"Perhaps I said it because I've been thinking of going back some time soon. Fifth Avenue is my Mecca, you know."

Bradford shrugged. "I'll take your word for it. I just wish I knew where he was."

"Did you hear he stole Sara Lynn's money before he took off?" I asked, instantly regretting the slip when I saw his face.

"She didn't say a word to me about it, and I was with her three different times today. What happened?"

"You know what? Maybe I was mistaken," I said, trying to backpedal as fast as I could.

"We both know better than that," he said. "Now tell me."

Lillian stepped in before I could tell him. "If you must know, Sara Lynn noticed that he'd taken five hundred dollars from their emergency fund and left an IOU. Sara Lynn couldn't be sure when he'd taken the money. Most likely it has nothing to do with what happened last night."

"Lillian, I might not be your biggest fan, but I know you better than to think you're stupid. Do you honestly expect me to believe the money vanishing isn't tied into Bailey's disappearance?"

"I don't expect anything from you," Lillian said. "I'm just giving you a plausible alternative to the conclusion you just jumped to. It could just as easily have happened that way."

He shook his head. "If you don't mind, I'll ask Sara Lynn if that's the conclusion she reached as well." His hand was on the doorknob when he said, "Oh, and do me a favor. Don't call her. I'd like to see what her honest reaction to the theft is without you coaching her."

Lillian shook her head. "I wouldn't dream of it."

After Bradford was gone, my aunt reached for my phone. "Who are you calling?" I asked.

"Your sister, of course," she said.

I reached over and hung up the telephone.

She stared at me and asked, "Jennifer, have you

lost your mind? I need to tell Sara Lynn he's on his way."

"Lillian, stop a second and think it through. Do you honestly think Bradford's going to be able to get Sara Lynn to tell him anything she doesn't want to? She's more stubborn than you are."

Lillian nodded. "I still think we should warn her that he's coming."

"And I think we've done enough already. I can't believe I told him about the missing emergency cash."

"Jennifer, you're just trying to help. So why do you think Bailey ran like that? It certainly makes him look guilty, doesn't it?"

"Do you think he'd actually do it?" I couldn't imagine my brother-in-law doing anything of the sort.

"People stopped surprising me ages ago," she said.

"Okay, let's see if we can help Sara Lynn out a more constructive way. You're talking to Polly and Luke. Should I tackle Kaye Jansen while you're doing that, or should I tag along with you?"

"Honestly, I don't know if either one of them would talk to me if you're right there. After all, your sister is the prime suspect, and we don't want any repeats of today."

"Hey, I already said I was sorry," I said, remembering my confrontation with Addie. "I can keep my mouth shut. I promise."

Lillian appeared to think about it a few seconds, then said, "I suppose you could be in the other room when Polly comes by to talk about the house. Short of slipping you in as a waitress, I don't know how I can get you close enough to my lunch date."

"Leave that to me." I knew I could work it out with Jack Hurley so that I'd be seated right behind Luke Penwright at the restaurant the next day. "So what do we do about Kaye?"

"We'll tackle her later if our other two leads don't work out," Lillian said as she stifled a yawn. "Now what can I do to help here?"

"You can go home and get a good night's sleep," I said. "We've got a busy day tomorrow."

"I don't mind staying, honestly, I don't."

"Good night, Lillian," I said as I pushed her toward the door. "I'll see you tomorrow."

"Fine, I can take a hint," she said as she left. I loved my aunt to death, but I didn't need her helping me pack. After all, I'd be the one putting everything away in my new place, and to do that, I needed to know where everything was in the boxes. I worked another half an hour before I found myself yawning, too, so I decided to call it a night. Oggie and Nash were curled up on my pillows, both of them sound asleep. I just wished I could drop off as quickly as they could, but I had a lot more on my mind than they did. As I finally nodded off, our suspects' faces were swirling around in my head, with one disturbing addition. Every now and then Bailey's face would pop up, only to fade away again. At least I hadn't seen Sara Lynn's face in the whirlwind. I would have never gotten to sleep then, if my subconscious mind was willing to admit what I wasn't ready to say out loud: that Sara Lynn surely had the required motive, means and opportunity to do away with Eliza Glade.

I felt like a criminal the next morning as I hid in Lillian's pantry waiting for Polly Blackburn to show up.

"Jennifer, can you hear me all right?" Lillian asked.

"I can hear you just fine," I said, "but I won't be able to see her face. I need to see her expressions if I'm going to be able to tell if she's lying or not."

"Sorry, I don't have any one-way glass for you to

peek through. . . . You know, that might not be such a bad idea. I could duck into the pantry and see what my guests are really up to behind my back."

"Lillian, could you be serious for one second?"

"Jennifer, I've never been more serious in my life." The doorbell rang, and she said, "Not a word out of you. I'll keep the door ajar so you can hear our conversation, but unless she's trying to strangle me, I don't want to see you come out of that pantry, do you understand? No matter how provoked you feel, you're going to have to keep your mouth shut. Can you do that? If you don't think you can, tell me now and you can slip out the back door."

The doorbell rang again. "Just let her in. I'll be quiet."

"No matter what?" Lillian asked again.

"Yes, now just go."

Lillian pulled the pantry door nearly closed, then I heard her high heels clicking on the hardwood floor as she went to let the realtor in. The only light I had was coming in through the narrow gap in the door. I was glad I didn't get claustrophobic.

Through the crack, I could see Polly as she walked into the kitchen. Her hair was dyed a shade of blond few people could naturally claim. She wore a dark blue suit, and a colorful scarf that added a blast of color. I could smell her perfume soon after she came in. Poor Lillian must have been overwhelmed by it if it was that strong in my confined space.

Lillian said, "Why don't you take a seat at the bar? This is my favorite room in the house."

Polly said, "I'll need to look around later, but we can certainly start here. I see you've got a fireplace in the kitchen. That's excellent, you know."

"I enjoy it," Lillian said. I could tell she was straining to keep her voice level. She had admitted that she wasn't a big fan of Polly, so I knew how hard it was on Lillian to make it appear otherwise.

I could see Lillian's foot from where I stood, and if I strained, I could barely catch sight of Polly's left arm.

"Lillian, do you mind if I ask why you're moving? I never thought you'd leave Rebel Forge."

My aunt said, "Sometimes one needs a change."

Polly jumped all over that. "Now, dear, you mustn't blame yourself for your relatives' actions. We all know you had nothing to do with what happened the other night."

"What exactly are you referring to?" Lillian asked.

"Why, the murder, of course. How difficult it must be to see your niece accused of the crime."

"I hadn't realized Bradford had made an arrest yet," Lillian said. I could tell without even seeing my aunt's expression that she was straining not to throw Polly out.

"Of course not, but everyone knows it's just a matter of time. So you've finally decided to go out on your own again. Jennifer must be crushed by your decision to leave her. From what I've heard, she wouldn't be able to run that little shop of hers without you."

"Jennifer will be fine," Lillian said. Her foot was nearly a blur, it was bobbing up and down so fast.

"Honestly, just between the two of us, she really did bite off more than she could chew. You're propping her up, aren't you? I can't imagine she makes enough on her own to buy food for those two stray cats she has, let alone pay rent."

Despite my promise to Lillian, I was ready to rush out of the pantry and let Polly say those things to my face. Lillian must have sensed it, too.

"Since we're letting our hair down," Lillian said,

"you must have mixed emotions about Eliza's murder yourself."

"Whatever do you mean?" Polly asked.

"Now that she's out of the picture, I can't imagine the chamber choosing anyone else but you to run the organization. It's rather convenient, isn't it?"

"I'm just as crushed as everyone else in Rebel Forge about what happened to Eliza," Polly said.

"I'm sure you are," Lillian replied. I doubted that Polly believed that she was being sincere. "So, have you already made your bid for her office, or are you going to wait a few days? You'd better not tarry, dear; you know how much power the president has."

"It's a great deal of work," Polly said. "In fact, I often helped Eliza with the day-to-day operations."

"Were you helping her the night of the banquet?" Lillian asked. "I understand the two of you had quite a discussion at Hurley's that night."

"That's utterly ridiculous," Polly said. "I don't know where you're getting your information, but Eliza and I got on wonderfully all the time."

"So you're claiming now you didn't fight with her that night?" What did Lillian know? If she had information about Eliza and Polly fighting, she hadn't shared it with me.

"We were discussing the award presentation," Polly said.

"From what I heard, you were talking about more than that. It was just before she died, wasn't it? You might have been the last person to see her alive."

"You mean besides the killer, don't you?"

Lillian hesitated, then said, "Tell me about the argument."

"I honestly don't know what you're talking about. If someone thought we were fighting, they were mistaken."

"How interesting," Lillian said.

"You don't believe me?" Polly said. "Do you honestly think I'd kill her to get control of the chamber? You must be joking."

"Polly, I want you to look at me. Does it look like I'm kidding?"

Suddenly the realtor stood, and I could see her face for just a second. "Lillian, I don't think you're serious about selling this place at all."

"Perhaps you're right," my aunt said. "Thanks for coming by, though."

"My pleasure," Polly said as she fled the room, and then the house. I waited for Lillian to come back, but after a minute I couldn't stand the suspense. I swung the door open and walked out of the pantry.

Lillian came back into the kitchen, a tight smile on her lips. "That was interesting," she said.

"I can't believe you let her sit there and talk about our family that way," I said.

"Jennifer, the only way I was going to get her to talk was by egging her on. I kept expecting you to break out of the pantry any second and hit her with a can of peas."

"They were green beans, actually," I said. "You did a good job holding your temper in."

"When you've been married as many times as I have, you get good at certain things, and holding your tongue is one of them. It's a shame you couldn't see Polly's face when I asked her for her alibi."

"That was slick, I'll give you that," I said. "How did she look?"

"Like I'd just stepped on her tail," Lillian said. "I might not have any proof she did it, but Polly certainly didn't do anything to encourage me to take her off our list."

"So it's lunch with Luke next, right?"

Lillian nodded. "It's set for one o'clock, so that will give us time to open the card shop and sell a few things first. Are you ready to go?"

I followed her out as she locked up, then I rode to the shop with her in her Mustang. Her last one had been wrecked, though not by Lillian, and I thought she'd try something different, but in the end, she'd gone with a nearly identical vehicle, down to the color of the carpet and the convertible top.

As she drove to Custom Card Creations, I said, "Does the entire town really think you're carrying my business with your checkbook?"

Lillian laughed harshly. "Jennifer, you can't believe one tenth of what that woman says."

"You didn't answer my question," I said.

"Who cares what they think? You and I both know that you're making it on your own. Does it really matter what the local gossip is?"

"It does to me," I said. "I'm still a little sensitive about the fact that you don't take a salary from the shop."

She glanced over at me. "Are you kidding me? I use more supplies than you'd ever have to pay me. I'm getting the bargain here, not you."

She pulled into a space near the shop, but not directly in front of it. As I started to get out, I saw that Lillian was staying in her seat. "Aren't you coming?"

"If you don't mind, I think I'll take the morning off. I want to do a little snooping before my lunch with Luke."

I glanced at my shop, then back at Lillian. "I can come with you, if you'd like."

She laughed. "Jennifer, I know you'd regret every second away from this place. Go on, run the shop, and I'll see you at lunch."

"Are you sure? I don't want you taking any chances without me," I said.

"Jennifer, I was watching out for myself long before you came into this world. I'll be fine."

"You'd better be," I said. "Who else could I afford to hire if something happened to you?"

She drove away, and I opened the card shop for business. Lillian had been right: I was exactly where I wanted to be. While I found a great deal of satisfaction in digging into the lives of the folks in Rebel Forge and helping unearth the truth, my first love was making and selling cards.

STENCILS AND STAMPS

A terrific way to jazz up your greeting cards is through the use of stencils and stamps. Most specialty craft and hobby stores carry a wonderful selection of each. Be creative with your ink to make the additions jump off the card. I like to shade the stamps and stencils I use with specialty marking pens. The results are beautiful, and all you need to do is color between the lines! Don't worry if your pen strays now and then. It just adds to the charm of your card!

Chapter 7

The door chime announced a customer, but I was just as happy to see my best friend, Gail, walk into the shop. "Hey, Jen. Any chance you could take an early lunch?"

"Would you believe it? I've got plans."

"Don't tell me you've got a hot date," she said.

I shrugged. "No, but Lillian and I are going to Hurley's, and I can't get out of it."

Gail shivered. "I don't know how you can go back there, especially so soon." She picked up a card, studied it a second, then put it back. "Listen, I wanted to talk to you about last night."

"It's okay, Gail, you don't have to apologize. After all, it's not your fault the guy didn't show up. Believe it or not, I had fun, anyway."

She bit her lip, a sure sign there was something she had to tell me, but didn't want to.

"Go on," I prompted her.

"What?"

"I know you've got something to say, and it's not exactly news you're glad to share. I won't get mad, I promise."

Gail laughed, but it was weak. "You know me too well. Okay, here goes. Reggie's not sure it's such a great idea that you move into the cottage." She expelled the words in a rush, and refused to make eye contact as she did.

"Yeah, I kind of got that impression last night. Helena thought it was a wonderful idea, though. Gail, is he giving you grief about this?"

She nodded. "Just a little. He thinks you took advantage of his mother."

"What's the matter? Does he think I'm not paying enough rent? Helena asked me what I was paying now, and when I told her, she halved it. Gail, that woman is lonely. She needs some company, and I need a place to stay. Unless you're totally against this, I'm going to go ahead and move."

She appeared to think about it a few seconds, then said, "Of course you should take it. It's perfect for you. I don't know what I was thinking."

I smiled at her. "Don't be too hard on yourself. The last thing I want to do is come between you and your boyfriend."

"I don't know how long that's going to last," she said. "I saw a side of him last night that didn't exactly thrill me. Then when he called me this morning demanding I talk you out of taking the cottage, I liked him even less. You know what? I'll help you move. How's that for sending a message of who I really support?"

"I'd never turn down the help," I admitted, "but you're just asking for trouble, aren't you?"

"Sometimes the world needs a little trouble to keep things alive."

The chime rang again, and I was surprised to see Kaye Jansen come in. She had a basket tucked under one arm, and it looked like she had chosen to visit my store on the one day I wanted to see her.

"Hi, Kaye, it's so nice to see you."

She looked startled by my enthusiastic greeting, and

I guess I could understand it. We'd never been all that chatty in the past, so I suppose I caught her off guard.

Gail said softly, "I'll see you later."

"Thanks for coming by."

After Gail was gone, Kaye approached me. "Jennifer, I hate to ask you this, but I'm taking up a collection from the Oakmont merchants for a floral arrangement for Eliza's funeral. Would you care to contribute?"

"Of course I would," I said, trying to sound as sincere as I could. "Let me get my checkbook."

I reached down to get my purse where I stored it behind the counter, and Kaye noticed my golden anvil.

"I must say, you didn't waste any time displaying it, did you?"

It took me a second to realize what she was talking about. "I'll come up with a better place for it later. To be honest with you, winning kind of caught me by surprise."

"You weren't the only one," Kaye mumbled.

"Excuse me?"

Her cheeks reddened slightly. "Goodness, did I say that out loud?"

"You did," I said sternly, "and I'd like to know what you meant."

"Jennifer, you must realize your choice wasn't unanimous among the award committee. After all, you barely qualified for it. I'm afraid there was so much heated debate, we had to shift our votes to anonymous ballots. Not everyone was pleased with the results."

I hadn't wanted the award, nor had I expected to win, but they'd given it to me. So why couldn't Kaye be more gracious about it?

"So which side was Eliza on?"

Kaye frowned. "She was your biggest advocate. I couldn't imagine why she pushed so hard for you—

not that you aren't deserving, but we did have other choices."

It was pretty obvious that Kaye hadn't been one of my biggest supporters. I wrote her a check for ten dollars—about all I could afford to withdraw from my anemic checkbook—but I didn't hand it over just yet.

"So I wasn't the only thing you two disagreed on."

That brought her head up with a snap. "Why? What have you heard?"

"Kaye, you've lived in Rebel Forge long enough to know that people talk." That was sheer bluff. I hadn't heard a word about her, but Kaye didn't know that. I tried my best to look like I was in on all of her dirty little secrets. The trick was trying to keep my mouth shut and letting her explain. That was one of the best ways to get an answer from someone who didn't want to talk. It was remarkable how most people hated silence, and were willing to fill it, even if it wasn't to their advantage.

I had to give Kaye credit. She held out nearly a full minute before she said, "Jennifer, it was all a misunderstanding. We settled our differences just before Eliza died."

Still silent, I arched one eyebrow and continued to stare at her.

"It's true," she continued. "I agreed to drop my suit, and she promised to stop spreading those rumors about the store." Kaye, her husband and her father-in-law ran a drugstore on the outskirts of town. So what rumors could Eliza have possibly been spreading? I'd have to ask around, now that I knew where to dig.

"I'm sure," I said, hoping she'd provide more.

"Well, do I get that check or not?"

"Certainly," I said as I handed it to her. Kaye

glanced at the amount, then said sarcastically, "Thanks so much for your generous contribution."

"You're most welcome," I said.

She stared at me a second longer, then beat a hasty retreat. Lillian and I certainly had more to talk about. If anyone could dig out the gossip on the rift between Eliza and Kaye, it was my aunt. I glanced at the clock and realized that if I didn't hurry, I was going to be late. Part of the plan depended on me convincing Jack Hurley to seat me where Lillian was going to be.

I slapped the BACK SOON sign in the door, then locked up and hurried to the pub. I just hoped that Lillian wasn't there ahead of me.

It was early enough that Hurley's wasn't crowded yet; early enough in the day, and the season as well. As soon as the main influx of tourists hit us, I wouldn't be able to get within fifty yards of the place. As it was, the faux Irish pub was half deserted.

Jack was behind the bar, cleaning his menus with a soft cloth. "Jennifer, it's good to see you."

Jack usually loved to tease me, but there wasn't a trace of humor in his voice. "What's wrong with you?" I asked.

"Can't I be polite to one of my best customers?" he said.

"Not if it's me. What's going on?"

He shrugged and threw the cloth down on the bar. "Things have been slow since the other night. I never should have let the chamber hire the place out. My wife told me it was a mistake, though she didn't know how epic it would turn out to be. I hope you're in the mood to eat a lumberjack's lunch. I could use the business."

"Sorry, about all I can afford right now is a salad."

Everyone kept telling me that once the full brunt of tourists arrived, I'd be swimming in money, but so far there was barely enough to dampen the soles of my feet.

"Then it will be the best salad you've ever had in your life." He stepped out from behind the bar and pointed me to a table.

"I've got a favor to ask," I said as I sat down.

"Name it and it's yours."

"Lillian is going to be coming in shortly with Luke Penwright. Is there any way you could seat them behind me?"

"What are you two up to?" he asked with a scowl.

"We're doing a little snooping," I admitted. I'd considered lying to him, but Jack Hurley had a strange effect on me. Whenever I was around him, I felt like an awkward teenaged girl again. It was all I could do not to giggle every time he talked to me, and I wasn't in any position to lie to him.

"Good for you," Jack said to my surprise.

"You're not mad that we're using your restaurant for our scheming?" I asked.

"Now, why on earth should I be mad? If you can find out what happened to Eliza Glade, I'll give you both free desserts for a year. It's amazing to me how someone could stab her in my kitchen during a banquet and not a soul witnessed it. If your brother doesn't solve her murder soon, I may be out of business."

"Is it really that bad?"

"Jennifer, I do well enough with the tourist trade, but it's the folks who live in Rebel Forge year-round who keep me going. I like my friends to feel welcome here, and right now it's as if there's a pall of death hanging over the place that's killing its spirit."

"I'm so sorry," I said. "I never even thought about how it would hit you."

He touched my hand lightly, and I felt it tingle, despite the fact that I knew the man had more children than I had cats. "You've grown into a sweet and kind woman, you know that?"

Before I could stop myself, a giggle escaped. "Thanks," I managed to mutter before completely embarrassing myself.

Jack smiled, but to his credit he didn't laugh. "Now let me see about that salad."

He headed off to the kitchen, and I was studying the furnishings when someone slid across from me at my table.

It was my ex-fiancé. "Greg, you can't sit there."

Greg Langston looked around. "Why? Is your date in the bathroom, or did he stand you up?"

"My, aren't you charming."

He scowled. "Come on, Jennifer, you're by yourself. There's only one place setting."

"I never claimed I was eating with anyone else. All I said was that you couldn't sit there."

At that moment, Lillian walked in with Luke Penwright. She looked surprised to see Greg sitting with me. Well, she couldn't have been any more surprised than I was. Jack came out of the kitchen, and if he noticed that Greg had joined me, he didn't show it. He led Lillian and Luke to their table, then handed Greg a menu.

"He's not staying," I said.

"Actually, I am." Greg yanked the menu out of Jack's hands.

"Jennifer, would you like me to reseat this gentleman?"

I saw Greg tense up, and it was pretty clear that

Jack was ready for a little distraction from his slow business. "It's fine," I said, trying my best to defuse the situation.

Jack shrugged. "Then it's all right with me. What can I get you?"

"I'll have whatever she's having," Greg said. I knew he hated salads, but out of sheer meanness, I kept my mouth shut.

Jack nodded and left. I could tell that Lillian and Luke were talking about something, but I couldn't hear much of what they were saying.

Greg kept trying to talk to me, when all I wanted to do was eavesdrop on my aunt's conversation. I had to brush him off if I was going to learn anything. "So how is Stephanie going to react when she hears we're having lunch together?"

"She'll just have to get over it," he said. "I've wanted to talk to you for a while now, but we never seem to get the chance to have a simple conversation."

"This isn't a good time, either," I said. "Can't we do it later?"

"We need to do it now," he said. "Jennifer, I thought Stephanie might be the one, but every time I'm with her, I keep thinking about you. We've got to resolve what's between us, so we can both move on."

There was a serious undertone to his words that was rare for him. "How do you propose we do that?"

"We need to go out on a date together, one last time, so we can put this behind us forever."

I was so startled by his suggestion that I nearly choked on my water.

"Are you all right?"

"I'm fine," I said, trying to catch my breath. "Do you honestly think a date will help us get past our situation?"

He smiled at me, and I felt my resolve weaken.

After all, how bad could it be, going out with him again? He'd always made me laugh, and when his hand brushed against mine, I could still feel the charge down to my toes.

"No," I said as emphatically as I could. "I can't do that anymore. Greg, we don't fit. Isn't that obvious by now?"

"So grant me this last favor. We go out, revisit our past, and then maybe we can both move on."

I looked at him intently. "What exactly did you have in mind?"

His words tumbled out. "I'm just talking about dinner. You don't even have to kiss me good night if you don't want to."

"Where?"

He met my gaze and said, "I was thinking we could go to The Chateau."

He'd named the most expensive restaurant in town. "Can you honestly afford that?"

Greg shrugged. "Why not go out in style, since it's our last date?"

Every ounce of my being was screaming no, so why did I say, "Okay. That sounds just crazy enough to work. When do you want to go out?"

"How about tonight?" he asked.

"Tonight is fine with me, but what is Stephanie going to say?"

Greg looked sheepish as he admitted, "To be honest with you, this was actually her idea. She thinks I'm still hung up on you, but Steph is under the impression that a date will clear it up once and for all."

"That's a first," I said. "I can't say I've ever had a date arranged by a man's girlfriend."

"So, should I pick you up at seven?"

"Why don't we just meet at the restaurant," I suggested.

"No," Greg said as he shook his head. "This is going to be a date, from start to finish. No cheating, okay?"

"Just as long as you remember that, too."

He had the decency to blush, but he was saved when our salads arrived.

"You ordered rabbit food?" he asked me.

"Try it. It's delicious."

Greg shook his head and spoke to Jack. "Can I get this to go?"

"No problem," Jack said as he took the salad away. He was back a minute later with a Styrofoam box, and after he handed it to Greg, he gave him the check as well. Greg paid and left, and I found myself watching him walk out the door, wondering exactly what I had agreed to tonight.

I was about to take a bite of my salad when I noticed that Lillian and Luke were gone.

"Can I get this to go, too?" I said after I waved Jack over to my table.

"Is it something I said?" Jack asked.

"No, but I've got to find Lillian. Did you happen to notice when she left?"

Jack scratched his chin. "She's been gone about five minutes. Luke looked like he was going to cry. What in the world was she thinking, bringing him here?"

"It was his idea," I said.

Jack put my salad into a container like he'd given Greg, and I asked for my check.

"I can't give it to you," he said, not even trying to hide his smile.

"And why not?"

"Your lunch date already covered it. What is it with you two, Jennifer? Are you on again?"

"Just for tonight," I said as I grabbed my salad and headed for the door.

I had the satisfaction of seeing the puzzled look on Jack's face as I left. He could join the club. I didn't have any more idea what I was doing than he did.

I found Lillian back at the card shop, and was surprised to see that she'd opened the place back up for business.

"Where did you run off to?" I asked her as I put my salad on the counter.

"I thought Luke was going to fall apart right on the spot. I had to get him out of there. I'm not surprised you didn't notice us, though. What was that all about?"

I wasn't ready to get into my social life with my aunt at the moment. "We can talk about it later. Did you get anything out of Luke?"

"Not in the restaurant, but out on the sidewalk he admitted that he was leaving town. He said being in Rebel Forge made him think about Eliza too much. My heart went out to the poor boy."

There was something about the man's behavior that I just didn't buy. "Lillian, did you ever consider the possibility that he's crying out of remorse for killing her? If he stabbed his ex-wife, leaving town might be his escape."

"I don't know," Lillian said. "I truly believe he loved her."

"You're nothing but a softie deep down inside, aren't you?"

She shrugged. "What can I say? I'd like to believe that all of my ex-husbands still carry torches for me. Why is it so hard to believe that Luke loved Eliza to the end?"

"Because she was fooling around with my brother-in-law, remember? I wonder if Bradford's had any luck tracking him down."

"I can't honestly imagine Bailey being that elusive, can you? We really should spend more time with Sara Lynn. It's not good for her to be alone right now."

I nodded. "Why don't you go over to Forever Memories this afternoon? I can handle things here."

"I wasn't talking about right now. Honestly, she's surrounded by the things she loves in her shop. Tonight is when she'll need us the most. What do you think? Should we make it another girls' night out?"

There was no way I was going to be able to keep from telling her the truth, so I decided to get it out of the way. But first, I wanted a little diversion. "I got a salad from Hurley's, and there's more there than I could ever eat. Why don't we split it?"

"That sounds wonderful," she said, "but you didn't answer my question."

"Why don't we eat first, then we can talk?"

It was obvious that Lillian thought I was up to something, but she didn't have a clue what it was yet. She retrieved plates and cutlery from the back room while I grabbed a couple of bottled waters from the refrigerator. After splitting the salad between the two plates, I realized that I still probably had more than I could handle.

I had to give Lillian credit. She managed to hold her tongue ten minutes into the meal before she started grilling me.

"So why can't you go out with us tonight?"

"I've got a date," I said, hoping she'd drop it, but knowing she never would.

"Is it the mysterious stranger from last night?" Lillian asked.

"No, it's Greg," I said. Maybe if I gave her short and simple answers to her questions, it would go quicker.

"You and Greg are dating again?" She sounded surprised by the notion. "I thought you'd written him off for good."

"I have," I said. "But his girlfriend thinks it will do us both some good if we go out on one more date so we can get it out of our systems."

"That is one understanding young woman," Lillian said.

"It's just dinner. Nothing more."

Lillian didn't look as though she believed it for a second. "And where is this dinner taking place?"

I mumbled the name of the restaurant, again hoping she'd let it go.

No such luck.

"I'm sorry, I didn't catch that. Where are you going?"

"The Chateau," I said, louder than I'd meant to. "He's taking me to the fanciest restaurant in Rebel Forge. There, are you happy?"

"The question is, are you, Jennifer? Do you really want to get Greg out of your system forever?"

I stabbed an errant lettuce leaf, then stared at it—impaled on my fork—for a second before I ate it. "Most of the time I think so, but then Greg does something charming and I find myself falling for him again. Lillian, I know you think we belong together, but I don't. And in the end, that's what matters, isn't it?"

My aunt patted my hand. "My dear, what you think is the only thing that matters. If you can't find happiness with him, then you should move on. Just be prepared for the consequences of your decision, though."

"What do you mean?"

She sighed gently, then said, "This woman wants him in her life, and she wants him all to herself. Sending you two out on a date is her desperate attempt to get all of Greg's attention, and not just some of it. Are you prepared to lose him forever?"

The finality of Lillian's words struck home. Was I really ready to let him go? He certainly found ways to upset me, but I had agreed to marry the man, not once but twice. What if we'd gone through with the ceremony one of the times we'd been engaged? Would we still be married, or would I have a failed attempt under my belt in my thirties. I honestly couldn't answer the question, and for the hundredth time, I wondered if going out with Greg again was the wisest thing I could do.

I suddenly realized Lillian was still staring at me. "I guess we'll see, won't we?"

"You'll do the right thing when the time comes, Jennifer. I have faith in you."

"I just wish I did," I said. "Enough about Greg. What are we going to do this afternoon to solve Eliza Glade's murder?"

"I was hoping you'd ask," Lillian said. "I've got a great idea about how to approach Kaye Jansen. It's going to be tough to get her to talk, but I think I know how to do it."

"She came by the card shop this morning," I admitted. In all honesty, I'd forgotten all about Kaye, given what had happened since her visit.

"What did she want?"

"She was taking up a collection for flowers. While she was here, I took a chance and asked her a few questions."

"Did you have any luck with her?"

I related what Kaye had told me, and I swear it was all Lillian could do not to rub her hands together with glee. "That's excellent work, Jennifer."

She got up and headed for the door. I asked, "Hey, where are you going?"

"I'm going to track down those rumors and see if any of them are true."

"And what am I supposed to do in the meantime?"

Lillian smiled at me. "Why, you make and sell cards, of course."

Before I could stop her, she was gone. It appeared that my aunt had ditched me once again, but I wasn't going to stand idly by, waiting for her to report back in.

There was some snooping I could do myself, and the best part was, I didn't even have to leave the card shop.

Chapter 8

At first I was afraid she wasn't there, but after ten rings, Savannah picked up the phone.

"Hey, it's Jennifer. I wasn't sure you were working today," I said.

"That's the problem. Things are hopping right now. Can I get you something to go, honey?"

"No. Listen, I'll call you back later when you're not as busy." I suddenly felt silly bothering her. Though it was true that Savannah had the best grapevine of anyone I knew in Rebel Forge, it wasn't fair to impose on our friendship.

"Now how on earth will you know that all the way over there at your card shop?" Savannah's laughter matched her personality perfectly: warm and joyful. "I've always got time for my friends. What can I do for you?"

"It's nothing, really. I was just wondering if you'd heard anything about Eliza Glade's murder."

"Do you honestly think folks around here can talk about anything else?" She lowered her voice as she added, "I'm afraid your sister's ears must have burned off by now, the way people are talking about her. I wouldn't blame her if she never left the house again."

"Have you heard anybody else's name mentioned as a suspect?"

"Jennifer Shane, what are you up to? Are you digging into another murder?"

"Savannah, I'm afraid if I don't, Bradford's not going to have any choice but to arrest Sara Lynn. That would tear my family apart. You know that, don't you?"

Her voice was suddenly soothing and motherly. "Now take it easy, child. Let me think about it a second. I've heard Addie Mason's name mentioned more than a time or two, and everybody knows how upset Luke was with his ex-wife. Let's see, one woman mentioned Polly Blackburn, but that's about it. Sorry I don't know more."

"Has anybody said anything about Kaye Jansen?" So far, Savannah had named nearly every suspect on my list.

"No, I don't think so, but that doesn't mean it didn't happen. I do my best, but some folks just don't talk loud enough for me to overhear them."

I heard her husband, Pete, call out to her, "Here's another order, Savannah."

She barely covered the phone as she said, "Then trot out here and deliver it yourself. I'm on the phone."

I walked over to the door with the telephone in my hand and opened it, just so Savannah could hear the chime. "Thanks for your time, but you're busy, and I am, too."

"I'll keep my ears open, Jennifer," Savannah said. "This is important."

"Thanks," I said as I hung up the telephone.

I felt better recruiting Savannah to our cause. She'd hear more of the gossip around town in an hour than

I would in a month, and now that she was helping out, Lillian and I could focus on the four people who had the most to gain from Eliza's death. Besides my sister and her errant husband, I amended silently.

Since there were no customers in the store, or even prospects on the sidewalk out front, I decided to go through my storeroom and collect some boxes for my move. I hated to leave Whispering Oak, but the cottage was going to be a neat place to live, even if Reggie wasn't excited about the prospect. That was okay with me. Helena more than made up for it with her own enthusiasm.

I was still amassing my collection of boxes when the front door chimed. I couldn't have been more shocked if the president himself had just walked in the door when I saw Addie Mason standing there with a gift bag in her arms.

"Hi," I said warily. "Listen, I'm sorry about before. I was out of line."

She shook her head. "No, I was the one who lost it. I came to say I'm sorry. Lillian helped me realize that I was just lashing out at you."

Addie handed me the bag, and I saw it was full of custom-made soaps and candles from her business.

"You shouldn't have," I said.

"But I wanted to." As she looked around my shop, Addie said, "I've always wanted to see how you make these wonderful cards. It's fascinating."

"I'd be happy to show you, if you've got the time. But who's watching your place?"

Addie's posture slumped. "I didn't have the heart to keep it open," she admitted. "It was probably insane for me to even come in today, but to be honest with you, I was afraid if I didn't go in this morning, I wouldn't be able to step inside the shop ever again. Crazy, isn't it?"

"No, it makes perfect sense to me. So what kind of card would you like to make?"

She looked as if she was ready to cry, but she managed to hold it in. "Can I take a rain check, Jennifer? I just want to go home, now that things are patched up between us. I never could stand having anyone mad at me. It's a character flaw, I guess."

"Hey, everybody wants to be liked," I said, though I wasn't sure it was true. Eliza Glade surely hadn't gone to much effort to achieve that.

As Addie started for the door, I said, "Hang on a second." I grabbed one of my basic card-making kits and pressed it into her hands. "If you feel like trying it later, this will give you something to do."

"I can't take this from you, Jennifer. That's not why I brought you a gift."

I smiled at her. "Don't worry, I promise it's not quid pro quo. I'd like you to have it."

"Thanks," she said, and before I could say another word, she was gone.

Now why did she have to go and be nice to me? I was all ready to go after her as my prime suspect, and she'd made a peace offering and set out an apology. It was going to be hard thinking of her as a murderer now. Then again, could that be the point? Had she come by my card shop with gifts in hand to diffuse my zeal? If so, it was a clever and devious act, more suited to her former partner than to what I knew of Addie. But it had worked—or at least it had before I suspected she might be playing me. I put the gift bag on the counter and tried to think about what Lillian and I should do next. I knew she was following her own line of inquiry, but so far I hadn't added much to the mix. I was still staring off into space when Lillian came back. I was surprised, when I glanced at the clock, to see that it was almost closing time.

"You've been gone a while," I said.

"Detective work takes time, skill, dedication and a gentle manner with people," she said. "Besides that, I stopped off and had a facial, too."

"Does that help you think?"

"No, but my skin feels absolutely marvelous. That's reason enough to pamper myself, isn't it? I wish you'd let me treat you to a day at the spa. It's wonderful, Jennifer."

"Thanks, but I'll stick with my oatmeal and olive oil scrub," I said.

"You don't know what you're missing," she said.

"And isn't it probably better that way? One day of pampering with you and I'd never be able to face my homemade scrub again."

"Perhaps you have a point," she conceded. "So what have you done this afternoon? Have we had much business?"

"It's been quiet," I said.

Lillian noticed the gift bag on the counter. "What have we here?"

"You're never going to believe this. Or maybe you will. Addie came by with a peace offering, and from the way she was talking, I have a sneaking suspicion that you were behind the whole thing."

"Nonsense," Lillian said. "Certainly we discussed what happened in her shop earlier, but I didn't say a word about her coming here to apologize."

"Then how did you know she apologized?"

"Why else would she bring you such a lovely gift bag, Jennifer? I trust you reciprocated."

"I gave her a beginning card-making kit," I admitted.

"That was exactly the right thing to do," Lillian said. "I'm proud of you."

"Don't rush your judgment," I said. "The entire

afternoon I've been standing here wondering if there was an ulterior motive behind her present and apology."

"Whatever do you mean?"

"Think about it, Lillian," I said as I picked up the bag. "What better way to throw me off her trail than by killing me with kindness? She knew why we were at her shop this morning. It was pretty obvious we're digging into Eliza's murder. Addie wanted us to think about her sympathetically."

I'd half expected a blast of scorn from Lillian, but instead, she laughed.

"What's so funny?" I finally asked.

"I'm sorry, Jennifer. It's just perfect. I've somehow managed to turn the sweetest young woman in Rebel Forge into a paranoid skeptic. My work is done here."

"You're not disappointed in me?" I asked.

"Are you kidding me? I couldn't be prouder."

What kind of family had I been born into, anyway? "You're insane; you know that, don't you?"

"I've heard the rumors," she said, "but I choose to ignore them. So, are you excited about this evening?"

"Why, what's happening? Oh, that's right. I'm having dinner with Greg."

Lillian said, "I certainly hope you'll be able to muster up more enthusiasm than that when he picks you up."

"I don't want to go at all," I said. "As a matter of fact, I think I'm going to go cancel this mistake before it goes any farther."

As I headed for the door, Lillian grabbed my arm. "I wouldn't do that, if I were you."

"Why not?" I asked, pulling away. "What possible good can come from this?"

Lillian took my hands in hers, something she'd done since I'd been a child. It meant she had a point to make, and wasn't about to give up until she made it. "Jennifer, you and Greg have been dancing around this for years. It's not healthy having things unresolved between you. Have you ever considered the possibility that you haven't been able to move on romantically because you still have such strong feelings for Greg?"

"That's utterly ridiculous," I said.

"Is it? Then you have nothing to fear tonight. If your love for Greg is as dead as you claim, then all that will happen tonight is that you get a free meal in the finest restaurant in seven counties."

"I still don't see why I should go through with it," I said. "But if it will keep you off my back, I will."

She released my hands, then said, "You'd better get going. I'll close up, and you can go get ready for your . . . evening out." It was pretty clear she'd wanted to say "date," but had thought better of it at the last second.

"Fine—especially if it's the only way I'm going to get you to drop this, once and for all."

If my aunt noticed the bite in my words, she chose not to comment on them. I left her at the shop and went home to shower and change clothes. Had I been protesting too much when Lillian had pressed me about my feelings for Greg? There was a great deal of history between the two of us, much of it good, but that didn't mean I wanted to go back and do it all over again. I hated to admit it, but his girlfriend was right. It was time for Greg and me to move on. My head kept telling me that, anyway, but my heart was another matter. There was something about that man—something I'd never been able to put my finger on, but real nonetheless. Intellect seemed to vanish when I was in his presence, and emotion took over. I'd just have to find a way to keep it in check tonight.

Then maybe, finally, we could both get on with our lives.

I fed the cats, then showered and dressed, just in time. I was putting the finishing touches on my makeup when the doorbell rang.

One last check in the mirror, then I answered it.

"Hi, Greg. Don't you look handsome." He did, too, wearing a charcoal gray suit I'd never seen before, and a burgundy tie that looked expensive.

He looked me up and down, then said, "I'd whistle at you, but I'm afraid you'd slap me."

"Go with those instincts," I said coolly, though for some reason I was happy he liked the way I looked. The red dress managed to hide most of my figure's flaws while highlighting the few assets I had.

"I've always loved you in that dress," he said as we walked down the steps to the front door.

"This old thing?" I asked, smiling despite my earlier promise to keep this light.

"You wore it to our last engagement party," he said softly. "Remember?"

Blast it all, I'd forgotten all about that. "I can change," I said. "Give me two minutes. Honestly, I didn't mean anything by it."

"Don't you dare. You look great," he said. "Besides, if we're late for our reservation, they'll give our table away."

"Are you sure? I don't mind. Honestly, I don't."

"Come on, Jen. If I let you go back in your apartment, I'll never get you out again."

We were just leaving the house when Barrett walked out of his apartment. He looked at us both before saying a word. Was that a touch of envy in his eyes? It was probably just my imagination, but I sincerely hoped not.

"Evening," he said.

"Good-bye," I countered, and Greg held the door open for me.

"What was that all about?" he asked once I was safely in his vehicle.

"Barrett has an overly generous opinion of his own charm," I said.

Greg laughed, and I asked, "What's so funny?"

"I miss your wit, Jennifer," he said.

"You didn't seem to miss it so much when you were dating Teresa Haywood."

"Hey, don't forget, that was after you broke up with me."

"How long did you wait to ask her out? Ten minutes, or did you show remarkable restraint and wait for fifteen?"

"As a matter of fact, Teresa asked me out. Is it my fault you were at Hurley's the same night we were there?"

I laughed, remembering the look of abject discomfort that had been on Greg's face that night. "You looked like a deer blinded by headlights. Whatever happened to Teresa?"

"She moved to West Virginia," he said.

"You seem to have a difficult time keeping your women," I said.

"Funny, it never was a trend until you came along," Greg said.

"What can I say? I'm special that way." As he drove us to the restaurant in his pickup truck, I said, "You know, we don't have anything to prove tonight, and I know you can't afford The Chateau. Why don't we go to The Lunch Box and eat there instead?"

"Are you kidding me? Savannah would never let you live it down that you were silly enough to go out with me again."

I touched his arm lightly. "Then let's go to Hurley's. I agreed to this farce, but I'm not going to put you in debt on my account."

"I can cover it," he said grimly. I knew how much his pottery shop made when the mass of tourists were gone, and we'd all gone through a lean winter, with summer nearly there.

"To be honest with you, I'd feel more comfortable at Hurley's," I said. "The Chateau is just a little too exclusive for my taste."

"Are you serious?" he asked.

"I am. Greg, let's at least have some fun, since this is the last time we're doing this."

Greg shrugged, then turned the truck around and headed for Hurley's. As he drove, I said, "You can take your tie off, too. I know it's got to be choking you."

"Come on, at least give me this much. Leave me with a little delusion that this night's special."

I said softly, "It is, because it's the last time we're going to do it. There's no pressure tonight, no final farewells or anything so melodramatic. Let's just be two old friends sharing a meal and some time together."

He nodded. "I've got to admit that sounds wonderful."

We parked in front of Hurley's. Greg jumped out to open my door, but I was too quick for him. Before I could get out, he said, "You're not playing fair. You never minded me opening doors for you before."

"Okay, I'll let you win, but just this once." I closed my door and waited for him to open it, but when nothing happened, I looked up to see him grinning at me. I was about to reach for the handle again when he popped my door open, and I barely managed not to tumble out onto the curb.

"You're out of practice," I said as I got out.

"I guess my timing is a little off," he said. "That's the story of my life."

We walked into Hurley's, and I was surprised that the place was only half full. Jack was frowning at his reservation book when he spotted us.

"We didn't call ahead," Greg said. "I hope you have room for us."

"You and a marching band," Jack said. He took in our outfits, then added, "My, don't you two look nice. Jennifer, if I weren't married with a zoo of kids, I'd ask you out myself."

"But would I say yes?" I said, fighting a losing battle to hide my smile. It never failed. Every time I was around Jack Hurley, I felt like I was fifteen years old, a freshman with a crush on a senior.

"There's no doubt in my mind, because I wouldn't give up until you did."

"Hey, in case you weren't sure, we're on a date here."

The tone of Greg's voice surprised me. Had the banter made him jealous?

Jack said, "Sorry, we were just teasing," as he led us to a table by the window, one of my favorite spots in the restaurant. "Beth will be serving you tonight, but in the meantime, can I get you something from the bar?"

After we ordered our drinks, Jack went away to make them, but not before pausing long enough to wink at me. I just shook my head and smiled.

Greg asked, "What was that for?"

"I just find it surreal being here with you tonight. So tell me about Stephanie," I asked. "She seems nice, and she's certainly pretty."

"Do we have to talk about her? I thought tonight was going to be about us."

I looked at him, but it was difficult to read his ex-

pression in the dim light of the restaurant. "Okay, if
it's a stroll down memory lane you're after, then I'm
your gal."

"Jennifer, at least try to act like this was a good
idea."

I suppose I had been a little hard on him. After all,
if I wasn't prepared to be gracious about it, I never
should have agreed to the evening out. I was still refusing to call it a date, even in my mind.

"I'm sorry," I said as I reached across the table to
touch his hand. I'd done it with no conscious volition,
just a habit resurfacing from the past, but I didn't pull
my hand away, and neither did Greg.

Jack slipped our drinks in front of us, then said,
"Beth will be right with you."

That broke the spell between us, and I picked up
my drink and I started to take a sip.

Greg said, "Hang on a second. We should make
a toast."

"Go ahead," I said, still rattled by the spark of
his touch.

"To us," he said simply.

I had no choice. "To us," I echoed, and we both
drank.

Beth showed up with the menus, and though she
wore a simple black skirt and white blouse, her rain-
bow hair coloring diluted the attempt at creating a
formal impression.

"Would you like a second?" she said.

"No, I think we're ready to order," Greg said. "Jen,
do you still like steak?"

"Slide one in front of me and we'll see," I said.
Usually I hated it when men ordered for me, but I
knew how much Greg liked to do it, so I let him.

After Beth left to place our order, I said, "You
enjoyed that, didn't you?"

He nodded. "Thanks for letting me order, and thank you for coming tonight."

"It's fun," I admitted, then I said, "If you'll excuse me for a second, I need to go to the ladies' room."

He stood as I did, and I was still laughing about his courtly manners when I walked toward the restroom.

I was nearly there when Jack approached. "Jennifer, I need to speak with you a second."

"Come on, you're a happily married man and I'm out on a date. We can't keep sneaking around like this," I said with a smile.

"This is serious. Someone outside needs to talk to you."

I followed him through the kitchen and out toward the loading dock. Before I went outside, Jack put a hand on my arm. "I'll be right here if you need me."

"What's this all about?"

He shrugged, and, after a moment's hesitation, I walked outside. I wasn't sure who I expected to see, but I was stunned nonetheless when Bailey stepped out of the shadows.

"Jennifer, thank God you were here tonight. I'm in some serious trouble. You've got to help me."

Chapter 9

I glanced over my shoulder to see if Jack was still there, but it was just the two of us standing in the dark. Great. My brother-in-law looked desperate, and, at that second, I wasn't entirely sure if it was safe to be alone with him.

"Bailey, what's wrong?"

His gaze scanned the alley behind us as he spoke. "Somebody's after me. That's why I took off like I did. Jennifer, I think I know who killed Eliza."

"Tell me," I said.

"I've got a feeling that I'm not the only one Eliza's been seeing lately. She told me something . . . No, I'd better not say it."

"Come on. I need to know, if I'm going to help you."

Bailey seemed to consider it for a moment, then he said, "I can't. It will be too dangerous for you if you know."

"Like I'm not in danger right now just standing here talking to you," I said.

He ignored that completely, and I knew not to push him on it. After a second, Bailey said, "Sara Lynn must hate me. Does she know I took our emergency fund?"

"You made it kind of obvious when you left every light in the house on."

Bailey stopped and stared at me. "Jennifer, when I left the house, it was completely dark."

"Then someone must have come in after you, and they didn't mind if the world knew it." I started looking out into the darkness myself. His paranoia, whether real or imagined, was catching.

"Oh, no, this is worse than I thought. I don't know what to do. You've got to help me."

"What can I do?" I asked. "I make cards for a living. You need to talk to Bradford. He'll know what to do."

"He's never liked me," Bailey said petulantly.

"Even if you're right, you're still family. I'm going to call him."

Bailey put a hand on my shoulder. "Are you sure?"

"Trust me." I dialed Bradford's number.

"Sheriff," he answered on the first ring.

"Hey, it's Jennifer."

"I thought you were out on a big date with Greg? Have you lost your mind, Sis?"

"Bradford, shut up and listen to me. This is important."

That certainly got his attention. "What is it?"

"I'm at Hurley's with Bailey. He says someone's out to get him, and I believe him."

Bradford's voice was calm as he asked, "Is he armed? Is there anyone else around?"

"What?" The questions didn't make sense.

"Jennifer, listen to me. I think he may have had something to do with Eliza's murder. If you can get help without alarming him, do it. If not, find a way to mollify him until I get there."

"Okay," I said, trying not to give anything away.

"Don't hang up. I need you to stay on the line so I know you're okay."

"We'll be waiting right here. I'll see you in a minute." Despite my brother's protests, I hung up the phone. I couldn't believe Bailey had anything to do with the murder, so I didn't want to give Bradford the chance to hang him based on something Bailey said when he didn't know my brother was listening in on our conversation.

"What did he say?" Bailey asked as I closed my flip phone. "Did he believe you? He didn't ask you any questions."

I'd never seen him so agitated. "Take it easy. He's coming here to help."

"I don't know. I think this is a mistake."

The next thing I heard was an explosion as a bullet ripped into the loading dock door behind us. The shot had gone between us, and I could swear I'd heard it whizzing through the air before I ever heard the gun's report. A second shot ripped the air above us, but by that time Bailey had tackled me to the dock and rolled us both off the platform onto the asphalt below. I was still trying to get my bearings when the restaurant door above me flew open.

My brother screamed, "Jennifer! Are you all right?"

"Get down," I shouted. "Somebody's shooting at us."

Bradford hopped down to the ground beside me and asked, "Where's Bailey?"

It wasn't until then that I realized my brother-in-law was gone.

"I don't know," I said. "He was just here."

"Take it easy. Were you hit?"

"I don't think so," I said as I searched my body for pain. I'd twisted my wrist in the fall, ruined a pair of brand-new pantyhose and wrecked my dress beyond salvation, but other than that, I was fine. "I'm okay."

"Good," he said as he patted my shoulder. Then he spoke into the mike hanging from his belt. "We've got an active shooter in the back of Hurley's. I need everybody here in two minutes with your lights on and your sirens blazing."

"What happened to those fancy codes you always use?" I asked after he was finished.

I could see a slight grin on Bradford's face. "I forgot to use them in all the excitement. That alone should get everybody's attention."

I stared out into the night. My eyes had grown accustomed to the darkness, and I searched the shadows for the shooter or Bailey. I couldn't see any other signs of life, but that didn't mean nobody else was out there.

"Why doesn't Jack turn the outside light on?" I asked. "Maybe we could see something then."

"And so could the shooter," Bradford said. "I told him not to."

I remembered the bullet hitting the door where Jack was waiting. "Is he all right? That first shot didn't hit him, did it?"

"He's fine. The thick wood of the door stopped the shot."

I was suddenly blinded as the first squad car pulled into the alley behind the restaurant. I was still trying to get my vision back when I heard more cars join us, along with the different squeal of an ambulance.

"Bradford, was someone hit? Why is an ambulance coming?"

"It's for you, Jennifer."

I started to stand and felt my knees give out on me. Luckily my big brother was there to catch me. "I don't need an ambulance," I protested.

"Well, you're getting one, anyway. I'm not taking any chances with you."

I started to protest when he held up a hand. "Jennifer, there are a couple of reasons we're going to do this my way. I want to be sure you're all right, and I also want the shooter to think he hit one of you. If he's cocky, maybe he'll slip up. So if you're not willing to ride in the ambulance for yourself, do it for Bailey."

I wanted to argue with him, but I couldn't. I drew the line at allowing them to strap me to a gurney, though. Unfortunately, nobody listened to my protests, and I was strapped onto one like a lunatic, not able to move my arms or my legs.

We were just about at the hospital when I remembered Greg. If nobody told him what had happened, I had a feeling he'd be under the impression I'd walked out on him. What a perfect ending to our long and troubled relationship.

Two hours later, I was back at the front door to my apartment. There was a wrap on my wrist, but other than that, I was as fit as I'd been before I'd taken that tumble. Thank goodness the loading dock was only a few feet above the pavement, or I might have been in some serious trouble. Bradford met me at the discharge desk and insisted on driving me home. My wrist was a little stiff, and I knew it would be even worse the next day.

To my surprise, Lillian was waiting for me inside my apartment.

"What are you doing here?" I asked her as Bradford led me in.

"Somebody had to feed your cats," she said.

"Did they cadge another meal out of you? I fed them before I left."

Lillian sputtered, "But they acted so hungry when

I came in, and this one kept mewing under the cabinet where you keep your cat food."

I picked Oggie up gingerly and said, "You should be in the movies, you're such a ham. I hope you're happy. You're getting fat, you know that, don't you?"

He offered me a brief mew, but he was too stuffed to squirm out of my arms. "Go on, you lunatic," I said as I put him down.

As he walked slowly off, Lillian asked Bradford, "Did she hit her head when she fell?"

"Not that the doctors could tell. Why?"

"I just don't think it's normal having a conversation with a cat. Of course she did the same thing before tonight, but I was still hoping they'd be able to do something for her."

"You're too funny," I said. "Thanks for coming, but I don't need a welcoming committee." As I looked around the apartment, I noticed that my neat piles were gone, and in their places were boxes, all labeled and sealed. "What happened here?"

Lillian looked sheepish. "Sara Lynn and I packed for you tonight. It was supposed to be a surprise. Surprise."

I'd deal with their invasion of my privacy later. "Where is she?"

Lillian said, "She's back at her place. After we heard what happened with Bailey, she insisted she had to go home in case he needed her. I tried to tell her that was the worst possible thing she could do, but she didn't listen to me. What a shocker."

I grabbed Bradford's arm with my good hand. "You've got to get someone over there. She could be in danger."

"Don't worry, Sis, I've got it covered. Lillian called me, and I sent Jody with Sara Lynn. The patrol car's in the driveway and he's sitting inside with her on my orders."

"Do you really think Bailey will show up with that kind of greeting?"

My brother snorted. "I don't think he's coming at all. He'd better not show his face around here. I may not wait for the judge to take care of his punishment."

"You honestly think he killed Eliza?" I asked.

"I'm not talking about that," Bradford snapped. "The fool put you in jeopardy, and then when trouble started, he left you there alone. I could kill him myself right now for that."

I touched my brother's arm lightly. "Bradford, don't forget, he saved me when he knocked me down. And how do you know he didn't go after the shooter when he disappeared?" I wasn't exactly sure what had happened myself, but I had to plant at least a little suspicion in my brother's mind that Bailey had done the right thing.

"He still shouldn't have involved you in this," Bradford said stubbornly.

"He was desperate. Bailey swore that someone was after him."

Lillian scoffed. "He's a delusional paranoid. The man never was all that stable."

"Then who shot at us?" I asked.

My aunt didn't have an answer for that. Bradford said sternly, "If he ever shows up again, call me and then get away from him as fast as you can."

"Isn't that what I did tonight?" I asked.

Bradford shrugged, then looked at my couch. "I'm sleeping here tonight."

"I'll be fine," I said.

"You sure will be, because I'm not leaving. Whoever took those shots at you might come back."

"They were shooting at Bailey," I said.

"How can you be so sure about that?" he asked.

For once, I didn't have a reply. Was it possible that I'd agitated someone enough to make them want me dead? Sure, I'd asked some questions, even pushed a few people for their alibis, but Lillian had been more active than I had and no one was coming after her.

"Those bullets had to be meant for Bailey."

"Most likely you're right, but we can't be too careful. Do you still have that sleeping bag in your closet?"

I nodded, and he headed to my bedroom to get it. "You can't babysit me around the clock," I called out.

Lillian smiled and said softly, "Let him think he's helping, Jennifer. He must feel terrible that he couldn't protect you tonight."

"How could he have possibly done anything to stop what happened at the restaurant?" I asked.

"He couldn't. That's the point. He's always watched out for you, and right now he feels he failed you."

My brother came out with my sleeping bag. "This is perfect," he said as he unrolled it on the couch.

"Shouldn't you tell Cindy you won't be home tonight?" If I couldn't convince him to go home, perhaps his wife could.

"Are you kidding me? It was her idea. She says I've been snoring too much lately, and she needs her rest."

"Fine, but if you wake me up, I'm pouring a bucket of water on you. It worked in third grade, and I'm willing to bet it will work again." I'd doused him once when we were kids, and though I could tell my folks approved of my intentions, they grounded me for a week nonetheless.

"I wouldn't try it," he said. "I sleep with a gun now."

Lillian said, "It appears that you two are settled, so I'm off."

"Should you be going home by yourself?" I asked.

"What if those shots really were for me? Do I need to remind you that you've been snooping into this more than I have?"

Lillian said, "And what makes you think I'll be alone?"

"What are you talking about? I didn't even know you were seeing anyone."

"Jennifer, I have more friends than Ben and Jerry. Sometimes Smith and Wesson come by, too, and with the five of us there to look out for one other, I'm sure we'll all be fine."

I looked at Bradford for help, and he said, "Lillian, I'll give you the couch if you let me have the sleeping bag."

She looked at the bag as if it were a large and hairy bug. "I'd rather take my chances with the mysterious marksman."

"If you won't stay here," I said, "at least go to Sara Lynn's house."

"I'm fine," my aunt said with a snap in her voice that I knew all too well.

"I'm not as worried about you as I am about my sister," I barked back at her. "She's alone, her estranged husband is in trouble and on the run, and she's rattling around in that big house all by herself. I don't care what excuse you make up, but you need to go over there right now. Think about somebody else, will you? She needs you."

Lillian studied me for a few seconds, then said, "Of course, you're right. I'll go there now. Good night."

I wanted to say something to lessen the blow of my harsh words, but all I could manage was my own good night.

After I dead-bolted the apartment door, I turned back to find Bradford appraising me with a steady look.

"What?" I asked.

"Sis, I've never seen anybody cow her like that in my life. Do me a favor, okay? Take it easy on me. I'm not sure at the moment that I'm on the right side of that dead bolt."

I picked up a pillow from the chair and threw it at him. "Oh, grow up."

He plucked it out of the air and hurled it back at me. "Now, what fun would that be?"

The next morning, I awoke to the smell of fresh coffee and pancakes. My brother was famous throughout the family for his flapjacks, and I felt my stomach grumble. I'd missed dinner last night, and then I'd been too exhausted to eat anything before bed. As I stood up, I felt a little stiffness in my wrist, but it really wasn't bad at all. I wouldn't be able to do handstands in the next few days, but I hadn't been able to do them all that well before I'd tumbled off the loading dock, so that was no great loss. I just hoped I didn't have to fight off anything tougher than a stuffed animal until my wrist healed completely.

I threw on a robe, and found my brother already dressed and dishing out a fresh pancake. "I hope you're hungry," he said as he slid it onto a plate, which he set beside a glass of orange juice.

"Is that freshly squeezed?" I asked as I sat down.

"It sure is," he said. "It says so right on the box."

I took a sip, then poured a little warmed syrup on the pancake and devoured it in record time.

He smiled at me as I looked up. "There's nothing wrong with your appetite, anyway."

"Just keep them coming," I said as he put another one onto my plate. "I missed dinner last night. I don't know what I'm going to tell Greg."

"You don't have to worry about him," Bradford

said. "We talked a bit last night when you were with the doctor."

"He came by the hospital to see me?" I asked, the bite on my fork temporarily forgotten.

"You can eat and listen at the same time," he said as he gestured to my food.

"Bradford, I'm serious."

"Okay, okay. I told him you were all right, and he said if that was true, he wanted to see you. For a minute there, I thought I was going to have to lock him up for disturbing the peace, but he finally listened to me. What is it with you two, anyway?"

"I wish I knew," I said. I wasn't looking forward to the conversation with Greg later. Knowing him, he'd want to reschedule our last supper together, but I'd had enough. I could barely manage to say no to him when I was at my strongest, and I wasn't anywhere close to that at the moment. Being shot at had that effect on me. No, it was time to end it with him once and for all.

Bradford glanced at the clock. "Is that time right?"

"Actually, it's five minutes slow. I keep resetting it, but somehow it keeps slowing down the exact same amount every time." I had a theory about my bumbling poltergeist messing with the clock, but I wasn't about to share it with my levelheaded brother.

He took the last pancake off the griddle and turned off the stove. "I've got to roll. Are you going to be all right?"

"I always have been," I said. "You're the one who insisted on giving me police protection. By the way, how did you sleep?"

"You tell me. Did my snoring keep you awake?"

"To be honest with you, last night you could have practiced bagpipes in the living room and I don't think it would have kept me up."

He laughed. "I'm glad to see you're in good spirits."

"I just hope Bailey's okay," I said.

"You still care about what happens to him after last night?"

"Bradford, he didn't mean to put me in jeopardy, I just know it. Has anyone seen him yet?"

He shook his head. "I checked in ten minutes before you got up. There's no sign of him anywhere."

There was something my brother was keeping to himself. I could see it in his eyes.

"What is it?" I asked. "What are you not telling me?"

"Jennifer, an arrest warrant's been issued for him."

I dropped my fork. "You actually think he killed Eliza Glade?"

"I need to talk to him, and it looks like this is the only way I'm going to be able to get his attention."

"That wasn't the question," I said.

"Blast it all, woman, you do your job and let me do mine, okay?"

"Okay," I said as I stood and walked gingerly to him. I kissed his cheek, a move that clearly confused him.

"What was that for?"

"Watch duty, a wonderful breakfast, looking out for your little sister. Take your pick."

He shook his head and laughed. "If I live to be a hundred, I'll never be able to figure you out."

"Call it my feminine mystique," I said.

"I'd rather call you nuts." As he walked to the door, Bradford said, "Lock this behind me, then keep your eyes open, okay? And don't push that wrist. You need to give it time to heal."

"Yes, sir," I said. It was all I could do not to salute, but I doubted he'd appreciate my humor.

After he was gone, I finished the last pancake, justifying it on the grounds that I'd missed dinner the night before, then I took a long, hot shower. I wished the apartment had a tub—a steaming soak would do me good—but I didn't have one here, or at my new address, either. Maybe I could talk Lillian into letting me borrow her Jacuzzi sometime. I took a quick shower, then after I dressed, I called Sara Lynn's place to see how the ladies had managed the night before.

To my surprise, Lillian answered the telephone.

"I'm really glad you stayed there last night," I said, wondering how my aunt's manner would be toward me this morning after our harsh exchange last night.

"Jennifer, how lovely to hear from you. How is your wrist?"

"It's good," I said, relieved my aunt had chosen to ignore what had happened. I'd been out of line with my comment, but then she'd made a few herself over the years, so I figured I was just catching up. Still, I'd have to watch what I said around her until the sting wore off. "Listen, I wanted to let you know that you can come in late if you want to. I'd be happy to open the shop by myself."

I knew that morning wasn't my aunt's favorite time of day, and I wanted to make the offer in recompense for the night before.

"Nonsense. Sara Lynn and I are commuting to work together this morning. I'm going to drop her off at the scrapbooking store, and then I'll be at the card shop."

"That's wonderful," I said. I wasn't sure how Lillian had managed to convince Sara Lynn to carpool, but I was glad she had.

"I'll see you soon, then."

After I hung up, I gave Oggie and Nash their morning meal, then headed out the door. My wrist throbbed as I touched the handrail. At least I didn't have to carry anything bigger than my purse. Then I remembered that I had to move soon, and I wondered how in the world I would manage it with a tender wrist.

When I got to my Gremlin, I was surprised to see Bradford sitting beside it in his squad car. "I thought you already left."

"I did," he said, "but I decided to come back. I'm taking you to work today."

"Bradford, don't be silly. I'm perfectly capable of driving myself to work and back."

"I know, but if something happens to you when I'm not around, Lillian, Sara Lynn and Cindy are going to take turns killing me. Come on. Get in."

I wanted to fight him on it. After all, I cherished my independence. I also realized that I'd feel better sitting beside Bradford in his squad car than I would all alone in my Gremlin. "Okay, but you'll have to pick me up after work, too."

"I'd be delighted," he said. Bradford let me off in front of Custom Card Creations, and just as I opened the front door for business, Lillian came in behind me.

Before I could say a word, she said, "Jennifer, we need to talk about what happened last night."

Oh, no, one of the two conversations I wanted to avoid more than anything in the world was about to happen. "I'm so sorry about the way I spoke to you. I was under stress—not that it's any excuse."

"What on earth are you talking about?"

I looked at her to see if she was joking, but she was dead serious. "I called you selfish and ordered you around last night. Surely you haven't forgotten that."

"Jennifer, you're much too sensitive. I don't recall you being harsh."

Fine. If that was how she chose to recall it, I wasn't about to set her straight. "Then what do we need to discuss?"

"Sara Lynn wants to see you immediately. She's still sitting in my car, as a matter of fact."

"What's so important?"

"She wants to talk to you about her husband, of course. It took every ounce of energy I had last night to convince her that you needed your rest. She kept demanding to talk to you. Do you mind speaking with her?"

"Lillian, I understand completely. I'll be right back."

"Take your time," she said. "I'll open the shop. In fact, why don't you two take a drive while you talk?" She stunned me by handing me the keys to her precious Mustang.

"Are you serious?"

"Of course I am," she said.

"Thanks." I left before she could change her mind. Lillian had been fanatical about keeping her last car to herself, and I gave up all hope of ever driving one when she'd had to buy a brand-new one.

As I got into the driver's seat, Sara Lynn asked, "What are you doing? I don't want to go anywhere. I want to talk."

"Lillian gave me the keys. I'm not about to pass this up. She said you wanted to talk. So talk." I started the car and pulled out, just narrowly avoiding a bread truck. He blared his horn at me, and I saw Lillian's head pop up in the front window. I waved at her and drove off, knowing without a doubt that this was the first and last time I'd ever get the chance to drive one of her cars. My wrist was tender as I held the wheel, but I managed fine.

Sara Lynn asked me, "What happened at the restaurant?"

"Are you telling me our dear brother didn't tell you a thing last night?" It was just like him, avoiding conflict where he could, when it came to Sara Lynn and me.

"I want to hear your version," Sara Lynn said. "I've heard Bradford's account, but now I want it all straight from you."

She had that right, after all.

After I shared every bit of what I could remember, Sara Lynn asked, "Who was he talking about? Did you get any hint of who he had in mind?"

I shook my head. "He wouldn't say, and I knew better than to push him on it. Do you want to know the truth? I honestly think he was more worried about your reaction to him taking your emergency fund than he was about someone trying to kill him. He loves you, Sara Lynn."

"Of course he does," she snapped. "That's why I don't understand how foolish he was with Eliza."

"Do you think you'll ever be able to forgive him?" I asked softly. I knew how much my sister believed in loyalty, and Bailey had crossed a line that was hard to forget or erase.

"I'm trying, believe me. I still love him. That's why he's driving me so crazy. I don't know what to do."

I wanted to pat her shoulder, to offer her a hug or something, but if I wrecked Lillian's car, she'd have my hide for a seat cover in her next Mustang. "Can I do anything to help?"

"I'm afraid no one can," she said. "Thank you for asking, though."

"I'm here if you need me," I said.

After a few moments, my sister said, "Actually, there is one thing you can do for me, Jennifer."

"What's that? Just name it."

"Find out who really killed Eliza Glade," she said. "That's the only way I'm ever going to be able to work this out with Bailey."

"I'm trying," I said.

"Then try harder. Would you mind taking me to Forever Memories? I need to be among my favorite things right now."

"I understand completely," I said as I headed for her store. I found great comfort in my card-making supplies, and realized it would be the same for Sara Lynn.

I pulled up in front of her shop, and she leaned in and said, "You've got to help Bradford find out who did this."

"I promise, I'll do my best," I said. But as I drove down Oakmont to Custom Card Creations, I couldn't imagine what I could do that I hadn't already tried. One thing was certain: whoever had shot at Bailey and me must have suspected that now I knew his secret, too. That meant that I'd have to be especially careful if I didn't want my name on the hit list as well. I had a strong feeling that if I found out who killed Eliza, I'd know who took those shots last night.

Chapter 10

Lillian was standing by the window, peering outside, when I drove up and parked in front of the shop. Before I could get out, she was there beside me. Her gaze scanned the paint job as I joined her and handed her the keys.

"That's one sweet ride," I said, grinning at her.

"Jennifer, you nearly gave me a heart attack."

"What are you talking about?"

"That bread truck," she said, nearly shouting.

"You're kidding. Lillian, he was the one who nearly hit me. Besides, it wasn't that close a call."

"You were near enough to smell his breath," she said.

"Would you forget about your car? It's fine."

She calmed down long enough to ask, "How's Sara Lynn?"

"She's pretty upset," I said. "She made me promise to find out who killed Eliza Glade, as if we haven't been trying to figure that out all along, anyway."

"Then we need to redouble our efforts," Lillian said. "And we will, just as soon as you take care of something else."

"What's that?" I asked, looking around the store. "Is there a customer I'm missing?"

"No, but we did have a visitor while you were gone.

Greg Langston was here, and he was determined to talk to you."

"Well, I'm not ready to talk to him," I said. One confrontation this morning was one too many, as far as I was concerned. Greg was just going to have to wait.

"Jennifer, you need to tie up this loose end so we can work without distraction," she said.

The bad thing was that I knew she was right. "Fine. I won't be gone long."

"I won't hold you to that," Lillian said.

"Trust me, what I've got to say can be handled in thirty seconds."

"It's not your opening statement I'm worried about," Lillian said. "It's his rebuttal."

"He's not talking me into anything else," I said. "I promise."

"Jennifer, you know how I feel about people making promises they can't keep."

"Just watch me."

I left the card shop and walked down to Greg's pottery store. If Greg wanted to talk to me, he was going to get more than he'd bargained for.

He was with a customer when I walked in. If I didn't know any better, I'd say that he'd planned it that way just to defuse my temper. I didn't care how irrational that sounded, even in my head. I wasn't in the mood to have anyone cross me, including my own subconscious.

The customer finally left, clutching two of Greg's kiln salamanders like they were made of gold. Greg took the partially melted and twisted triangular cones used to gauge the temperature in his kiln, added a few features like legs and a face, glazed them, then retailed them to the public as small knickknacks. "I sell more of those than I have any right to, especially since they're basically free to create. Jennifer, I honestly tried to get to you last night, but your family wouldn't let me near you. I'm so happy you're all right." He gestured toward my wrist tenderly. "Are you all right? Were you scared?"

"What? No. Yes, of course I was. Listen, we need to talk."

"I came by your shop a little while ago," he said, "but your aunt told me that you were with Sara Lynn. How's she holding up?"

I shook my head. "Greg, right now we're talking about us. You and me, for the last time there will ever be a you and me. Last night was the biggest summation of our relationship that there could ever be. Anybody who thinks God or Fate or whatever Supreme Being they believe in doesn't have a sense of humor is insane. We can't even have a farewell dinner without it being interrupted by gunplay. If that's not a sign, what is?"

Greg stared at me a few seconds, then said, "I believe it was a sign, too. Just not the same one you think."

"What are you talking about?"

"I don't think we should have ever broken up," he said, his words coming out in a rush. "Think about it, Jennifer. There's a reason we didn't finish this between us."

"Yeah, some lunatic took a couple of shots at me." My voice was shriller than I liked, but I couldn't help it. "Greg, we don't belong together, not anymore. I loved you at one time, I've never denied it, but there's no future in this relationship for either one of us."

He stepped closer than I would have liked, but I didn't back away. "Jennifer, look into my eyes and tell me you don't still love me."

I felt his presence, a strong aura that made my

knees go weak. "It's no use," I said, but even I was aware of the lack of conviction in my voice. "I can't do this."

"You're right," he said, stepping even closer. "There's no use fighting it anymore."

It would have been easy enough to turn my cheek as he started to kiss me. I'd done it enough times in the past to be an expert at it. But I didn't even move, I'm sorry to say. Ten seconds into the kiss, I'd forgotten why I'd come there in the first place. I'd also forgotten my name and my birthday. Wow. I was about ready to give in completely, regardless of the consequences, when Greg's front door opened. As he pulled away from me, I caught a glimpse of Stephanie's back as she ran back out the door.

And then Greg gave me the only real answer I'd been expecting all along. If he was really interested in being with me, he would have at least said something to me before he raced out after her. Instead, all I heard were his pleas to Stephanie to stop. He didn't even look back at me as he bolted down the street after her.

I shook my head, trying to wipe the images I'd been entertaining out of my mind. At last I knew that whatever Greg and I had shared was finally dead. It still stung as I saw him race through traffic to catch the woman he loved. More than a little part of me was sad that I wasn't the one for him, though I knew in my head that he wasn't the one for me, either. There was no denying we had a physical pull between us, but that was all it was, and I refused to try to build anything more solid on just that. I needed more, and to be fair, I was sure that Greg did, too. It was finally time to move on.

I couldn't exactly lock his shop up, since I didn't have a key, but I did the next best thing. I flipped his sign to the closed position, then turned off all the lights. It would have to do until he got back. Waiting there for him was out of the question. I just hoped he understood what had transpired between us as clearly as I had.

I walked back into the card shop and Lillian was about to say something when she must have caught the look on my face. Without a word, she stepped up to me and wrapped me in her embrace. No doubt we looked ridiculous, with me towering over her and trying to bury my head in her shoulder, but I didn't care. I let my tears out, and the ferocity of the outburst startled me. After I'd cried for a few minutes, I pulled away. "Wow, I haven't cried like that in ages."

"You were past due," Lillian said. "I gather it didn't go as smoothly as you'd hoped."

"It was awful," I said, dabbing at my eyes with a Kleenex. "He kissed me."

"Was it really that bad?" Lillian asked, obviously surprised by the admission.

"No, that's the point. It was so good it curled my toes."

"So what's the awful part?"

"Stephanie caught us, and he ran after her without saying a word to me. It's over. It probably has been for a long time—I've known that in my head—but my heart's just catching up with the fact."

"I'm so sorry," Lillian said. "Give it some time, and you'll feel better. Would you like to go home early today?"

"No, thanks," I said. "As a matter of fact, I'd like something to throw myself into. Like a murder investigation."

"Jennifer, are you certain that's what you want to do?"

"I've never been more sure of anything in my life," I said. "Let's get started."

Lillian got out our whiteboard and erased the day's specials we'd tried last week. Every day we'd offered a different discount on something, and it hadn't been worth the time it had taken to come up with the specials. Perhaps it would work when we had more foot traffic in the store, but it was a bust this time of year.

I took a soft cloth and erased the board so we could start fresh. I replicated the listings we'd done on her mirror at home a few nights ago.

"Do we have anything new to add?" I asked as I studied it.

"I'm not sure how the shooting fits in, or Bailey's mysterious stalker," Lillian said.

"I'm not, either. So who do we tackle first?"

She tapped the board under Addie's name. "Why don't we look at motives? She gets the shop. That's got to be worth a fortune. Is greed a big enough motive?"

"You'd better believe it," I said and wrote that single word under her name. I wished I had a green marker to write it in, but our St. Patrick's Day blowout had turned into a flop, and I'd killed the marker in the process.

"So how about the others?" I asked as I studied the list.

Lillian took a red marker and wrote LOVE under Luke Penwright's name. "And the others?" I said, gesturing to Polly Blackburn and Kaye Jansen. "I've got it," I said as I wrote ENVY down for them.

Lillian studied the list, then said, "We're covering our share of the seven deadly sins, aren't we?"

"One of them is usually behind every murder, wouldn't you say?"

"It's always a good place to start," she said.

I tapped the closed marker on my chin. "There's something that's been bothering me. Bailey said something about another man in Eliza's life, and I don't think he was talking about her ex-husband. Could this mystery man have killed her when he found out about Bailey?"

"It's possible, but who do we put down?"

I made a big black x on the board, and wrote LOVE under it. Lillian studied the addition, then said, "So let me get this straight. We know that one of these people probably killed Eliza, including our mysterious stranger. And we think we know the motive, but it's a multiple choice question instead of a true or false exam. Does that about sum it up?"

I threw the marker down. "It's hopeless, isn't it?"

"I wouldn't say that," Lillian said. "But we do have a way to go before we make anyone the least bit nervous."

"So what do you suggest?"

Lillian thought about it, and so did I. Finally, she said, "If we can eliminate one of our suspects because of logistics, we might finally get somewhere."

"Gotcha. I'll talk to Kaye and Polly to see if they've got alibis."

"Jennifer, I can do it."

"Honestly, I don't much feel like being around here right now," I said. I was afraid Greg would come back, and I didn't want to talk to him until he had a chance to get his emotions in check. "Please?"

"Fine, but be back here by three. I have something I simply must do then."

"I'll be back in plenty of time," I said. "So what's so important?"

"Jennifer, if I'd wanted you to know, I would have been a little more specific, now wouldn't I?"

"Be like that, then. I'm out of here."

As I walked toward Kaye's shop, I couldn't help wondering what my aunt was up to. It would be tough getting it out of her, since she could keep a secret with the best of them, but if I was determined enough, I'd find out sooner or later.

For now, I wanted to forget all about Greg and that kiss so I could focus on who killed Eliza Glade.

I wished I had my Gremlin, but it was back at Whispering Oak, since Bradford had dropped me off at work earlier that morning. It would be more trouble than it was worth to pick up the car. Besides, it was a beautiful day, and I needed the exercise. I walked along Oakmont, keeping my gaze down as I went past Greg's pottery shop. I thought about popping in on Sara Lynn, but I had nothing new to tell her. Maybe I'd have more when I came back through.

I found Kaye working the front cash register at the drugstore. She was busy helping a customer, and I doubted she'd even seen me come in. During the busy summers, I knew she always hired her niece to help out, but for now, it was a skeleton staff, with her up front and her husband covering the pharmacy in back of the store. Thad was quite a bit older than Kaye, and it was rumored around town that her heart had been enamored more with his net worth than his love. Before my mother died, she'd always said that people who married for money earned every penny of it, and I hadn't really understood what she meant until years after she was gone. I'd heard that Kaye had been shocked to learn soon after her marriage that it was her father-in-law who really owned the place, and not her bridegroom.

She was selling a tourist a digital camera as I walked in, but I noticed that she didn't ring up the sale. Instead, I heard her tell the customer, "I can't give you a receipt since our register's not working. But if you have any trouble at all, bring it back to me and I'll take care of you."

"Small towns," the man said. "You just have to love them."

After he was gone, Kaye saw me and asked, "Jennifer, what brings you here? Did you decide to contribute more to the fund? I'm still taking donations."

That was a cheap shot, clean and at the knees. I had to give her credit for so viciously attacking me with a smile on her face.

"Actually, I was hoping I could have half of it back," I said before I could stop myself.

She looked stunned by my words.

"I'm kidding," I added, but she still wasn't sure how to take it. Good. I wanted her off balance.

"So what can I do for you?"

"I was wondering where you were just before Eliza was murdered. I didn't see you at your table, and I'd wanted to ask you where you got that dress you were wearing." That was nothing but a bald-faced lie. The only reason I would have asked her where she'd bought it was so that I would never shop there myself. It looked like a bridesmaid's dress with a hangover, with more ribbons and bows than a county fair.

"I had it made for me exclusively," she said proudly.

No doubt by a blind seamstress. "So where were you?" I smiled as I asked her, but it didn't take the heat from my question.

"I'm sure I was right there."

"And I'm sure you weren't," I said. "And that's what I'm going to tell my brother." Lillian would have been proud of me. She'd taught me that when they called your bluff, you raised over the top to drive them out.

"Let me see. Oh, yes, that's right. I'd stepped outside to have a smoke. You can ask Polly. She was there with me."

"Did anyone else see you two?" I asked.

"No, it was just the two of us. Jennifer, are you snooping around again? You know you shouldn't."

"We all have our vices, don't we?"

I left before she could get another jab in. I headed straight to Polly's realty office so I could ask her the same question I'd just asked Kaye.

Sure enough, she backed Kaye's story completely before she ducked out the door to show a house on Hickory Street. Fancy that. Either they were both telling the truth, or the two women had conspired to alibi each other. Did that mean they were guilty of anything more than a nicotine habit? I couldn't see them agreeing on where to eat lunch, let alone on killing Eliza Glade, but it was still a possibility. I'd managed to waste most of the day tracking down leads and taking a walking tour of Rebel Forge. I'd have to grab a quick bite before I headed back to the card shop, since Lillian had her mysterious errand to run. But I needed to see how my sister was doing first, and if that made Lillian late, then that was just too bad. After all, she had been the one drilling it into me from birth that family came first, and the whole world had to take second place.

I still felt a little uneasy going into Forever Memories. After all, I'd been working there part-time right up to the day when Sara Lynn had turned down my card-crafting idea and I'd walked out to start my own business. My job as a corporate sales rep peddling dog food had been completely unsatisfying, but working at Sara Lynn's with all those tools, stickers, papers and stamps had been my true love. It was wonderful that they all applied as much to card making as they did to scrapbooking.

Sara Lynn's shop was well stocked with many of the same supplies I carried, but my sister had arranged things in a completely different way than I had. I liked a lot of her ideas, but I'd been hesitant to borrow her displays without permission, and I wasn't comfortable asking. I noticed she'd recently added a workstation where people could use a custom letter-cutting machine.

"That's new," I said as I saw Christy Keystone behind the register.

"The customers really love getting their hands on the equipment. We've sold more machines in the past two weeks than we did the four months before it."

It appeared that my sister didn't have the same compunction about borrowing that I did. I would have been stunned if she hadn't gotten the idea for the demonstration area from me. Maybe I'd return the favor and steal some of her better ideas. After all, at least we were keeping it in the family.

"It's so nice to have you back," Christy said. "I've missed seeing you every day."

"How are you, Christy?"

"Haven't you heard? I'm going by Chris now. It seemed silly for a woman my age to keep being called Christy."

"Chris it is," I said. "Is my sister around?"

She frowned. "No, she's gone for the day."

"Did something happen?" I asked.

"No . . . at least I don't think so. She said there was something urgent she had to take care of, and then she took off."

Oh, no. I wondered if it had anything to do with

her errant estranged husband. "Do you know if it involved Bailey?"

Chris looked shocked by the suggestion. "I didn't think so. No, I'm sure of it. This had to be something else."

"I'm calling Bradford anyway," I said. "Can I borrow your phone? The battery's low on my cell, so I turned it off."

"Sure thing," Chris said as she scooted the telephone toward me.

I dialed Bradford's cell number, and when he answered, he was out of breath. "Yeah?"

"What have you been doing, chasing down criminals?" I asked.

"Something like that. What's up?"

"I'm at Sara Lynn's scrapbooking shop, but she's not here. Bradford, I'm worried about her."

He paused a moment, then said, "Hang on a second, would you?"

"Okay," I said. As I waited for him to come back on, I let my gaze drift around the shop. Sara Lynn had a knack for display that I envied, and I promised myself I'd do a better job at the card shop once things settled down. If they ever did.

He came back on. "Sorry about that. Don't worry about Sara Lynn."

"I can't help it. I'm afraid she's with Bailey."

He laughed. "I doubt that, since I'm looking at her right now."

"What have you two been doing, racing each other around the town square?"

"How did you know? Listen, did you need to talk to her?"

I thought about it. Was there really anything I needed to share with my sister? She was with Bradford, so I knew Sara Lynn was all right.

"No, just tell her I'll talk to her later."

"Will do," he said, and before I could ask him what they were up to, he hung up on me. I'd been meaning to remind him to pick me up after work, but I'd have to call back later. I walked back to my card shop, and when I got to Greg's business I saw that the lights were back on. He was sitting at the counter, and on an impulse that was against my better judgment, I walked in.

When he looked up, it was pretty obvious he'd been hoping I was someone else. "Hi, Jennifer."

"I've had warmer welcomes in my life," I said. "Did you ever catch up with her?"

"No, she was too fast for me. Sorry I ran out on you like that."

"Greg, you have nothing to apologize for."

"Not even that kiss?" he said, giving me a sheepish grin.

"Kiss? What kiss?"

"If you don't remember it, I didn't do a good enough job."

I smiled. "Actually, you're even better at it than I remember. It's almost a shame we won't get to do it anymore."

There was silence for a few moments, then he said softly, "You're right. It's over, isn't it? I guess I knew it in my heart, but seeing Stephanie run off like that tore me apart. She's who I belong with, Jennifer, not you."

"I couldn't agree with you more," I said, "though it's not an easy thing to hear. I hope you can fix things with her."

"Me, too."

He didn't sound like he had much hope. "If there's anything I can do, let me know."

"I think we've both done enough, at least together," he said.

"As long as we're clear that whatever we had is gone," I said, needing the closure of that final admission.

"Agreed," he said. "But as corny as it sounds, I still want to be your friend."

"I don't think it's corny at all." I approached him and stuck out my hand. "Let's shake on it."

We did, and I started for the door. "Jennifer?"

I turned back. "Yes?"

"Thanks. For everything."

"Even this afternoon?"

He smiled. "Yes, even for that. Stephanie will come around, especially if I apologize enough."

"Then you'd better get to it," I said, "because here she comes."

Stephanie didn't even break stride as she walked into the pottery shop. Ignoring Greg for a moment, she faced me and said, "If you think I'm giving him up without a fight, you're nuts."

"Believe me, he's all yours," I said. "What you saw was a good-bye kiss, nothing more."

Stephanie frowned. "It looked more like hello to me."

I looked at her intently. "I promise you this. You don't know me, but I keep my word. Ask anybody. You have nothing to worry about from me."

She acted like she couldn't believe it.

Greg said, "It's true."

She iced him with a glare, then turned back to me. "Are you sure? I know about your history together."

"That's just what it is: history," I said. "But we're going to be friends, and I won't give that up without a fight, either."

Stephanie smiled slightly. "I think I can handle that."

"Good," I said as I stuck out my hand. She looked surprised by the gesture, then shook my hand. I was glad she hadn't wanted to arm wrestle for Greg. That girl had a grip on her.

Greg said, "I'm glad that's settled."

Stephanie stared at him a second. "You're kidding, right? Do you honestly think I'm letting you off the hook that easily?"

"I was kind of hoping you would," he said.

I laughed as I headed for the door. "Good luck."

"Thanks," Greg said.

"I wasn't talking to you."

I felt good as I walked to the card shop. It was going to be an adjustment changing my attitude toward Greg, but I had a feeling it would make my life a lot less complicated having him as a friend instead of a sometime love. Maybe I could even start being nicer to him again.

Stranger things had happened.

Chapter 11

"What did you find out?" Lillian asked as I walked in the door.

"You're not going to believe this, but Polly and Kaye are acting as each other's alibis. I didn't even realize they were friends."

"I heard they couldn't stand each other," Lillian said.

"So it's unlikely that they conspired to kill Eliza together, isn't it?"

Lillian frowned. "That depends."

"On what?"

"Whether they hated Eliza more than they do each other."

"I don't know which is more likely," I said.

"Maybe we should do a little more digging." Lillian looked at her watch, then said, "But not now. I've got to go."

As she started out the door, I asked, "Are you sure you don't want to tell me where you're going?"

"Positive," she said, and then I was alone. The shop was quiet for most of the afternoon, so I decided to copy Sara Lynn's display techniques and show the steps to making a simple double-fold card with window cutouts. My wrist was sore, but I could still work through it. Besides, it was the best therapy, physical and emotional, for me. I had samples for each step and was ready to mount them onto cardboard backs when the phone rang.

"Custom Card Creations," I said.

"I never get tired of hearing you say that. You sound so professional," Gail said.

"It's all an illusion," I replied as I glued one of the cards to a bright orange piece of cardboard. "What's happening?"

"I was hoping we could hang out a little tonight, but I've got to go out of town for a few days," Gail said.

"Don't tell me Reggie's taking you to Cancún."

Gail sighed. "At this point, I'm not even sure he'd take me to a convenience store for a Coke and a Zinger."

"Trouble in paradise?" I asked as I mounted another card sample. I was the queen of multitaskers. Well, at least the princess.

"Honestly, he's been distracted lately, and I'm wondering if he's been seeing someone else."

"You're kidding. What man in his right mind would two-time you?"

"My point exactly," she said. "Anyway, I'm not sure if we're going to date anymore."

"I hope I didn't make it worse by moving over there," I said. "It's still not too late if you want me to back off."

"No," Gail said. "That cottage sounds perfect for you. Don't worry about me. I'm sure someone else will come along."

"There's no doubt in my mind," I said. She hadn't mentioned the shooting last night, and I wasn't sure if I should bring it up myself. After all, there was nothing either one of us could do about it at the moment, and I didn't want to worry my friend unnecessarily.

I was just about hang up when she said, "I can't

believe you weren't going to say anything about what happened last night."

"So you heard?"

"Jennifer, all of Rebel Forge knows. Why didn't you call me?"

"I didn't want you to worry," I said.

"Too late for that. Are you sure those shots weren't meant for you? I know how you like to snoop. Maybe you got too close to somebody."

"If I did, it was purely by accident," I said, laughing.

"Be careful, okay? I couldn't afford to lose my best friend."

"I wouldn't want you to lose her, either," I said.

"Well, I'd better go," Gail said. "I've been dreading this sales call. The guy's a real Neanderthal."

"I'm sure you can handle him."

"Oh, I can handle him, all right, but I'd like to make the sale, too."

"Just consider it a challenge," I said.

"Jennifer, they all are."

By the time I was ready to close the shop, I had the display finished and mounted to the wall by my card kits. It looked really nice, but I felt a little guilty stealing Sara Lynn's idea. I'd have to say something to her before someone else did. I just hoped she'd understand.

I waited outside for five minutes before my brother showed up. Since he was my ride, I hadn't had much choice, though my wrist was starting to bother me again. All I wanted was to go back to my place, grab an ice pack, take a few aspirin, and flip on an old movie on television. Okay, a pizza would be nice. And some Coke. But that was it. Then again, I'd love a piece of chocolate cake for dessert. It was probably all a little self-indulgent, but I figured I was due. I could really use some comfort food.

Bradford drove up wearing street clothes and driving his pickup. At least he had the courtesy to hold the door open for me as I got in.

"You're late," I said.

"Sorry, I got tied up with something. I hope you weren't waiting long."

"Five minutes," I admitted. "So what have you been doing? And why are we in your truck and not your patrol car?"

"I took this afternoon off," he said.

"With a killer loose in Rebel Forge?"

"This couldn't wait till later," he said.

As he started driving, I said, "Is there any chance your dear, sweet wife has any chocolate cake lying around?"

"If she does, she's better at hiding things than I am at finding them. Would you like me to stop someplace for you?"

"Honestly, I'm in the mood for some pizza and some cake, but it can wait. Right now all I want is to get home and relax. Bradford, that was my turn back there." My brother had completely blown past the path that led to Whispering Oak.

"Trust me, I know what I'm doing."

"Listen, big brother, you're going to cancel whatever it was you had planned. I'm not in the mood for any surprises this evening."

"Then you're not going to be very happy," he said softly.

"We're not going to your house, are we? I'm fine on my own. Honestly. Just take me home."

"That's what I'm doing," Bradford said.

I turned around and pointed. "It's back there, remember?"

"Not anymore," he said. "What do you think I've been doing all afternoon? Sara Lynn, Lillian and I moved you out of Whispering Oak, including Oggie and Nash."

"You what?" I screeched. "I wasn't even finished packing."

"We took care of it for you," he said. "I'm sorry, but your car's still parked there. I'll take you over to pick it up tomorrow."

"I can't believe you did this." It was just like my family, butting in and offering help when none was needed.

"Believe it," he said. "It was Sara Lynn's idea, and I wasn't about to say no. She had a good time, and it seemed to get her mind off her problems, so be gracious, would you?"

"Maybe I did overreact a little," I said. "It really did help her?"

"The only thing that would have made it better would have been if you were there, too, but part of the kick for her was doing this as a surprise for you."

"Okay, I'll be gracious," I said. "But it's going to be a stretch."

"Did you think that was a news flash? I've known you longer than anybody should."

He paused at the gate of my new place, then punched in a set of numbers. As he drove in, he chose a path I hadn't seen earlier. "Do I have my own entrance?"

He laughed. "I guess in a way you do. They can't even see you come and go at the main house. I think it was designed that way on purpose. You've got more privacy than anybody needs here. The way it was situated, it wouldn't surprise me if they couldn't even see your lights from the house."

"I like that," I said.

"I knew you would." He stopped in the trees just before we got to the cottage. "Listen, we all worked really hard on making the place feel like home. It would help if you could smile once or twice, even if you're not feeling it."

"Got it. Fake it till I make it."

"Jennifer, you know what I mean."

I wanted to pat his shoulder, but my wrist really did hurt. I doubted it would be healed by the time I would have been evicted, so my family really had helped me out. I just wished it would have been at my bidding and not theirs.

As Bradford pulled up in front of the place, Sara Lynn and Lillian came out to greet us.

"Surprise!" they shouted.

"It's that, all right," I said. "You all really shouldn't have. It's too much."

Sara Lynn hugged me, and I noticed that she was being careful of my wrist. "Nonsense. We were happy to do it. It looks lovely," she added.

"I can't wait to see it. How do my roommates like it?"

Lillian smiled. "You're kidding, right? There are so many places to swoop down from, they both think they've gone to cat heaven."

I walked inside and took it all in. They'd done a marvelous job, even adding fresh flowers to the small dining table in the kitchen. "Those are beautiful," I said as I saw the skillfully arranged roses, baby's breath and ferns.

"Thanks," Bradford said.

"You picked them out?" I asked.

"Hey, I'm not completely without taste."

Lillian and Sara Lynn looked at me, but nobody said a word. Bradford said, "I don't get any respect in this family."

I kissed his cheek. "Thank you, it was thoughtful of you to bring me flowers."

"Okay, it was Cindy's idea, but I picked them out. Well, I picked them up, anyway. She ordered them and had them waiting for me at the florist."

We all laughed, including Bradford. Lillian asked, "Would you like some company tonight, or would you like to settle in by yourself? You won't offend us if that's your preference, I promise you."

"I'd love to have a housewarming party," I said. "Just not tonight. My wrist's aching, and I just want to grab a bite and go to sleep early."

"That's fine," Sara Lynn said. "We'll do something next weekend, once you've had a chance to settle in."

Lillian nodded her agreement, then said, "There's a pizza in the oven, and we took the liberty of stocking your refrigerator. I hope you don't mind."

"No, I think I can live with that," I said, smiling. Okay, maybe it wasn't such a bad thing being the baby of the family. Sometimes it was nice being pampered.

I walked them outside, and Bradford said, "I'll pick you up bright and early."

"I'll let you come get me on one condition," I said. "We go get my car so I don't have to rely on the kindness of strangers to get back and forth from work."

"You're calling your dear, sweet brother a stranger?" he asked.

"Bradford, I've known a lot of people in my life, and they don't come any stranger than you."

Lillian and Sara Lynn laughed, and the three of them got into the pickup and drove off. I went back inside, feeling good about my family, and what they'd done for me. Nash was on one of the beams in the kitchen, swishing his tail as he watched me. "So, what do you think?"

He didn't comment, but he looked happy enough to be there. I was alarmed when I couldn't find Oggie, then I spotted one paw hanging down from the loft. The little rascal was already asleep on my pillow. Trust my cats to land on their feet, no matter what the situation was. I just hoped I'd do as well. The place looked smaller with my things there, and I wondered how I'd manage, but rearranging would have to wait for another night. For now, I just needed some peace and quiet.

I was jarred awake by a pounding on my cottage door, and for just a moment, I incorporated it into my dreams, imagining someone was driving nails into my car's roof.

From outside, I heard Bradford's voice, and realized it was real. The cottage was pitch black, and I nearly fell out of the loft as I climbed out of bed. My robe was on a nearby chair, and I hastily wrapped it around me as I answered the door.

"Bradford, what's wrong? What time is it?"

"It's a little after three," he said. "Get dressed, Jennifer."

"Can you tell me what this is about?"

He looked so sad it nearly broke my heart. "Somebody just burned down Whispering Oak."

Five minutes later, we were in his squad car heading back to my old apartment. Bradford had supplied coffee for both of us, and I took a sip of mine, trying to wake up. I could see an orange haze in the sky, diluted by black smoke. "What happened? Do you know yet?"

He shook his head as he drove grimly through the night. "There will be time for that later. Right now they're just trying to put the fire out."

I nodded. "Will they be able to save the house?"

He shook his head. "I doubt it. It was blazing

pretty fiercely by the time somebody called it in. It was an anonymous tip from a cell phone, and the voice was so distorted it could have been a man or a woman."

"You're thinking it was deliberately set, aren't you?"

"What makes you think that?" he asked.

"I'm here, aren't I? I doubt you'd drag me out of bed unless you were afraid of something like that."

"You're right, it's exactly like that," he said.

There were two fire trucks at the scene when we got there, and Jody—one of my brother's deputies—was keeping everybody but emergency crews out. Bradford stopped near his deputy and asked, "Anything new?"

He looked at me, then down at the ground. "Yep."

"What is it?" Bradford asked. "She's going to know soon enough."

"They found a body inside," he admitted.

Oh, no. As much trouble as I'd had with Barrett, I still didn't want to see him dead. Why hadn't he moved out a day early? For that matter, I was suddenly very glad that my family had relocated me and my cats.

"You okay, Sis?" Bradford asked me.

"No, but I will be."

He nodded, then said to Jody, "Keep everybody out of here."

"Including the press? Kyle Gaston was here from the newspaper, and when I told him he couldn't go back there, he started screaming about a lawsuit and freedom of the press."

"What did you do?" Bradford asked him.

"I told him when they started giving his newspapers away, then he could squawk about free press, but until then, there were safety issues."

Bradford smiled. "I bet he loved that."

"Yeah, well, you know."

My brother nodded, then drove on. The smell was worse than the smoke, though there was plenty of that. The fire department had managed to kill most of the flames, but every now and then I could see a flare-up in the ruined shell of the place I'd just lived. One wall was partially standing, and the roof had collapsed in on it. Everything was blackened, and I coughed from the smoke.

"It's bad, but believe it or not, you get used to it after a while."

"I don't think I want to," I said. My Gremlin was still parked in front of the house, but something was wrong. It wasn't until I was closer that I realized someone had broken out the driver's side window.

"Did that happen in the fire?" I asked.

"No, they had to move it pretty fast to get the fire trucks in. Sorry. I'll have it taken care of tomorrow. Today, I mean."

"It doesn't matter," I said. "Do you think they've moved the body yet?"

"No, they have to wait until the coroner gets here. Jen, do you have any idea who would do this?"

"Of course not," I snapped.

"Don't react. Take a second and think about it. Who would want Barrett dead enough to kill him? We're working on the assumption that it was him until we get confirmation, since he was the only one left. I talked to the guy as we were moving your stuff. It's rough."

I thought about Barrett's girlfriend, Penny, and how volatile she could be, but that didn't make sense. He was moving in with her. Unless Barrett had changed his mind. "He's got a girlfriend with a temper," I said. "Her name's Penny. That's all I know."

"Describe her," he said.

"She's petite, a blonde, somewhere in her midtwenties."

"Penny Hale," my brother said. "It has to be her."

"You actually know her?"

"I'm the sheriff here, Jennifer. I know most of the folks in Rebel Forge. Let me make a phone call. I'll be back in a minute."

Bradford left me standing there, staring at the remnants of Whispering Oak. I hadn't lived there long, but I'd fallen in love with the place. I wanted to feel bad about the ruined building and all of the lovely furnishings that had been in it, but all I could think about was poor Barrett. We'd shared a connection, a spark that might have led to more if Penny hadn't barged back into his life when she did. As I stared at the house, the final wall collapsed, sending sparks and billowing clouds of smoke into the air.

Bradford came back, shaking his head.

"What's wrong?" I asked.

"I just called Penny."

"How did she take it?" It was a telephone call that must have been torture for my brother to make.

"She put him on the phone. Whoever that is in there, it's not Barrett."

"What? It couldn't be Jeffrey. He moved out days ago."

"Any chance he came back for something?" Bradford asked.

"It's possible, but Barrett told me he was gone for good. You don't suppose it's Hester, do you?" She was the landlady who had so unceremoniously kicked us all out, and while she wasn't going to get my vote for citizen of the month, she didn't deserve what she got.

"It's a man. That much we know. The rest is up to

the coroner. Let's get you back to your cottage. I just thought you'd want to see this."

"You're right. I would have never forgiven you if you hadn't gotten me."

We drove back to my cottage, and I could still smell the smoke from the house. It was on my clothes, in my hair and in my lungs. After my brother dropped me off, I took a long, hot shower and scrubbed until all traces of the smell were gone. I buried my clothes in the hamper, and, with my hair still wet, I crawled back into bed, doubting that sleep would come. So, if it wasn't Jeffrey or Barrett, who had died in that fire tonight? Was there another ghost on the property now, or was that legacy over with the demolition of the building? I said a silent prayer for Frances Coolridge. While most people would have laughed if they knew I was serious, Frances and I had found a way to cohabitate—an absentminded poltergeist and an equally distracted live woman in her thirties. When she hadn't been trying to kill me, she'd made an amusing roommate.

I woke up with a start later in the morning, surprised that I'd been able to get to sleep after all. The cats awoke as if nothing had happened, and I didn't want to spoil their delusions. If they'd missed me during the night when I'd been with my brother, they didn't show any sign of it.

"How do you two like our new place?" I said as I watched them dig into their bowls. There was no reply, not a single acknowledgment that they'd even heard me. What a shock: my cats were ignoring me. As they ate their light morning meal, I joined them with a bowl of cereal of my own, and then I got dressed. I wasn't sure how I was going to get to work, since my plans to pick the Gremlin up had been shattered, along with the driver's side window. I was still wondering how I was going to get to town when Lillian showed up.

"Good morning," she said, the second she saw me, then hugged me so tight I could barely breathe. For a little woman, she had one whale of a grip. "Jennifer, I'm so happy you're all right."

"No happier than I am," I said. "How did you know I needed a ride?"

"Bradford called me," she said. Though the two of them had been feuding for years, it was good to see that they were finally working things out. "Are you ready to go?"

I said good-bye to Oggie and Nash, then locked the door. "Let's go."

As we drove to the card shop, I asked, "Did they find out who was in the house?"

"From what your brother told me, they're hoping to make an ID today." She shivered slightly as she added, "I can't quit thinking that might have been you."

"And it would have been, if you all hadn't moved me yesterday. Did I thank you for all of your hard work?"

"You did," Lillian said. "I just can't imagine who would be in there. Oh, Bradford wanted me to tell you that he got in touch with Jeffrey. He's hale and hearty, so that's another name off the list. It was most likely some indigent. How in the world he found out so fast that the house was empty is beyond me."

"I'm just glad it wasn't anyone I know," I said.

As we drove, Lillian said, "Jennifer, have you considered the possibility that the fire was meant for you?"

I hadn't even entertained the notion. "You're kidding me, right? Who would want to kill me? I haven't annoyed anyone in weeks, at least not that much."

"Think about it. Bradford and I discussed it this morning, and I think he's right. Whoever started that fire thought you were at home."

"What makes you say that?"

"Your Gremlin was parked in front of the house, remember? It's only logical that the arsonist thought you were home."

"You keep saying the fire was deliberate," I said. "Is there any proof that it wasn't an accident?"

Lillian nodded. "They found signs this morning that an accelerant had been used inside the building. It's pretty clear the fire was set on purpose."

That information sent chills through me. "If Bradford is so worried about me, why isn't he here?"

"Jennifer, your brother has one murder to solve, and now most likely two. He can't babysit you the entire time. But don't worry. He promised me he'd have someone keep an eye on you."

I'd been under surveillance before by the Rebel Forge police department, and it hadn't worked out all that well for me in the past.

"Still, short of locking you up in a cell so he can keep an eye on you, he's doing the best he can do."

I stared at her as she pulled up near the card shop. "Since when did you become such a big fan of my brother's?"

"I don't know what you're talking about," she said.

My aunt had the most selective memory I'd ever seen in my life, but if she wanted to pretend everything was fine and dandy, that was all right with me.

"I want you to open the shop this morning," I said.

"And what are you going to do? It's too dangerous for us to keep snooping into Eliza's murder."

We were still in front of the shop when I said, "It's too risky not to. If you're right and someone was trying to kill me last night, do you think they're just going to give up when they find out I survived the fire? I have to find them before they find me. It's a matter of survival now."

"Then I'm coming with you," Lillian said. "Let's just make a sign that we're closed until further notice, and we can track this killer down together."

I touched Lillian's arm, and was glad my wrist was nearly healed. "Lillian, as much as I appreciate the thought, you need to keep the card shop open."

"Jennifer, this is no time to worry about missing out on a few sales. There's something much more important at stake here than your shop's bottom line."

"Think about it, Lillian," I said. "If the killer sees the shop is open, then he won't come looking for me around town. I honestly think that the store is too visible for anyone to make a run at me here. The best way for you to help me is to make it look like we don't suspect a thing. If you're afraid to stay here by yourself, though, I completely understand."

"You know I'll help in whatever way I can, Jennifer. Don't forget that the fire department already knows the fire was set on purpose, though."

"Does the killer know that? Would we, if my brother didn't happen to be the sheriff? I think we've got a small window here to figure out who did this before I have to go into hiding, and I'm not about to squander the chance."

Lillian nodded reluctantly. "I see your point. So then who do you talk to first?"

"The person who had the most to gain from Eliza's death," I said. "It's time Addie and I had another little talk."

MAKING YOUR OWN PAPER

Making paper is much easier than it looks. All you need are a few simple items like some "seed" paper—newspaper, copy paper, tissue paper or a blend—a frame, some paper towels and a blender. Cut your base paper into one-inch squares, then put them in a blender with water to make a slurry. Pour the mix out into your frame, which can be as simple as a picture frame with plastic screen mesh stapled to it or as fancy as a kit frame. Press the water out of the mix, pull out your sheet and let it dry. There are countless variations, but the basic steps are easy to master. One warning, though. You might want to use an old blender, as this process is tough on the appliance. I bought one just for papermaking, and it works great. This is especially fun to do with kids.

Chapter 12

"We need to talk," I said as I walked into Addie's shop.

"Jennifer?" She looked shocked to see me, but quickly covered it up. "About what?" Addie asked. I didn't know if she meant to, but her tone perfectly matched mine. The niceties were gone, which was fine with me.

"You know perfectly well what I'm talking about. Don't play around with me."

Her gaze narrowed as she stared at me. "Jennifer, I thought we patched things up between us. Do you really want to battle with me?"

"There's something you should know," I said. "I'm not afraid of you, and a little fire isn't going to stop me."

She looked startled by the accusation. "What are you talking about?"

"Are you honestly trying to tell me you don't know what happened at Whispering Oak this morning?"

"I heard sirens, but I had no idea what they were about. I just figured some drunk had plowed into a tree again. It happens all the time in tourist season."

"It's not tourist season yet," I said. "So what do you have to say for yourself?"

"You know what? I don't care for your tone of

voice. If you're not buying anything, you need to leave."

I looked around her shop, then shook my head. "No, thanks. There's nothing here that's worth the money."

It was a low blow, but I didn't care. I may not have known who Eliza's killer was, but that didn't mean I couldn't stir things up. I figured if the killer got mad, he might get sloppy. If that meant that I angered four innocent people along with one guilty one, I was more than willing to make amends later.

For now, it was time to spread my own seeds of destruction and put the town of Rebel Forge on notice that I wasn't going down that easily.

Next on my list was Kaye and her drugstore. I walked there with a fierce stride, daring anyone to cross me. On my way into the drugstore, Reggie—Gail's boyfriend, or ex—nearly knocked me over coming out. "Jennifer? What are you doing here?"

Why was everyone so surprised to see me? "I have an errand to run," I said. "How about you?"

"I needed to pick up some medicine for my father," he explained. "I'm glad I ran into you. We need to talk."

"Sorry, I don't have time right now."

I tried to brush past him, but he wouldn't budge. "You can't move into the cottage," he said. "I won't allow it."

"I know you're not happy about the arrangements, but it's between your mother and me."

"Not if I make an issue of it. And you'd better believe me, I'm going to. I'd like the key back."

I laughed at him, though I probably shouldn't have. "You're too late. I moved in last night."

He was startled by the statement. "What? I didn't

realize . . . It doesn't change anything. You still have to move."

"When your mother tells me that, I'll go," I said. "But not before."

He stared at me, then brushed past, dismissing me with a glare. If Reggie thought I was going to be that easy to evict, he was sadly mistaken. Helena was another story altogether, but I'd have to hear the words from her lips, and I didn't think she would ever say them.

Kaye was at the front checkout. "Jennifer, thank goodness you're all right. I can't believe that lovely old building is gone. The historical society has been trying to get it designated as a landmark for years, and I honestly believe we would have succeeded this time. Whoever burned it down should be executed."

She couldn't fake the ardor in her voice. Kaye's declaration took the steam out of my step for a moment. "Do you have any idea who would be capable of doing it?"

Kaye looked shocked by the question. "No civilized person, that's for sure. I just don't understand why. How did you manage to escape?"

"I moved out yesterday afternoon," I said.

"How fortunate," Kaye said, then her eyes narrowed. "You were displaced unwillingly, weren't you? I bet it infuriated you."

"Wait one second," I said. "If you're suggesting I had anything to do with that fire, you're nuts."

"I'm just saying, some people may think that's how it looks, Jennifer."

"Then let them say it to my face," I said. "Do you have any suspects besides me?"

"I didn't mean to make it sound that harsh," Kaye said.

I waved a dismissive hand in the air. "Forget about it. Well, do you?"

"No, I'm sorry, I don't."

I started for the door as Kaye asked, "Where are you going now?"

"I need to speak with Polly," I admitted.

"You can't. She stopped by here yesterday afternoon. She was on her way to the Outer Banks." The banks were a popular vacation destination for folks from our part of Virginia. While we had beaches of our own, the chain of islands on the North Carolina coast were particularly lovely, especially the parts not infested with summer rentals and T-shirt stands. I could still remember the open stretches of windswept dunes from my childhood, and the last time I'd been there a few years before, it had been difficult believing it was the same place. Too many people with too much money were ruining one of the country's most beautiful and delicate habitats, and it didn't appear that anyone was doing anything about it.

"Did she say how long she'd be gone?" I asked.

"Just a few days, I think," Kaye said.

"I'll talk to her then," I said.

Kaye wasn't finished, though. "I'm guessing Luke Penwright's on your list, too, isn't he?"

"Why do you ask?"

"Jennifer, I make it my business to know people. You're speaking to everyone your brother interviewed the night Eliza was murdered. Don't bother denying it."

I grinned at her. "Okay, I won't. Do you have any idea where I can find Luke?"

"You just missed him. He's on his way out of town. For good, from the way he was telling it."

Blast it all, I needed to talk to him. If he was running because he thought he'd been successful in killing me, I had to dissuade him of that notion. I knew Bradford couldn't hold him, but if he left for good, my brother might never be able to find him again.

"Thanks," I said as I raced out the door.

To my surprise, Kaye followed me outside. "Try the Petrol Planet. He said he had to gas up first, and I'm willing to bet he's still there. He's driving a forest green motor home."

"Why are you helping me?" I asked her.

"You may not believe this, but I hope you figure out who killed Eliza. We weren't close—far from it, actually—but I don't want people in town whispering behind my back for the next thirty years that I was one of the suspects in the case."

"I'll buy that," I said. Then I remembered I didn't have my car. "Any chance I could borrow your car?"

Kaye shook her head. "Sorry, but I'm not willing to help that much."

I raced toward Sara Lynn's shop, hoping that she was there. If I couldn't borrow her Honda, I was out of luck.

"It's an emergency. I need your car," I said breathlessly as I ran into Forever Memories.

Sara Lynn reached into her purse—tucked safely behind the counter—and tossed me her keys.

"Don't you want to know what I'm doing?" I asked.

"Tell me when you bring my car back."

I had to look twice to be sure it was my sister and not some imposter. It was a sure sign that she'd been shaken up by last night's events, since there was no doubt in my mind that Bradford had already brought her up to speed on what had been happening.

I raced toward the gas station, and sure enough, the motor home was still at the pump.

As I pulled in behind it, I changed my mind at the last second, and swerved so I could keep it from leaving before I was ready. I got out and saw Luke coming out of the cashier's office.

"Jennifer, you really should slow down."

"I will as soon as I have the time. I was hoping I'd catch you. I heard you were leaving town."

He nodded. "There are just too many bad memories around here for me. Now that Eliza's gone, there's no reason for me to stay."

There was a group of men standing by the entrance, and I felt like Luke had said it for their benefit, not mine. If he wanted to put on a play in public, I was game.

"Funny, I never thought of you as a coward."

He gave me a hard look; the men standing around had dropped all pretense that they weren't listening to every word.

"You'd better be careful there, Jennifer."

"What are you going to do, attack me? Like some-one attacked your ex-wife?"

His face reddened at my goading, and I saw one of the men flinch. "That's enough," he said when he could control his voice.

"I don't think so. If you loved Eliza as much as you claim, you surely wouldn't run away with your tail between your legs if there was a chance her killer might be caught. Don't you want to be there when Bradford brings him in?"

I saw a few nods out of the corner of my eye, and I could see that I was scoring some points. Luke must have noticed it, too.

"Do you really think your brother's capable of catching anything more than a cold?"

"Look at his track record," I said. "He's good at what he does." I was on solid ground there. Bradford was the best sheriff Rebel Forge had ever had, and more folks said it than me. "I can't believe you're just giving up. I thought you were a real man."

He actually took a step toward me as I said that, and I could see the pure hatred in his eyes. Only the sight of the men standing by watching kept him from approaching me more. I thought he was going to come after me anyway when one of the men, an older fellow named Moss Marlette, said, "She's got a point, Luke. What's your hurry?"

That emboldened one of the other men to say, "I knew your daddy, and he never gave up a day in his life."

Luke wanted to scream, I could see it in his eyes, but instead, he plastered a fake smile on his face and said, "You know what, Jennifer? You're right. I'm turning this rig around and parking it back at Campers' Cove, and I'm not leaving until the worm that killed my Eliza pays for it."

Several of the men nodded their approval, but out of their hearing, Luke added, "This isn't over."

I nodded. "Anytime."

I drove off after making sure that Luke was heading back into town. I'd found the right button to push, but it hadn't been that hard. I loved Southern men dearly, but they were so proud, a lot of the time it made them predictable. I wasn't all that thrilled with my own behavior, but I couldn't rule Luke out as a suspect if he wasn't around. I was making quite a name for myself as a hag around town, but it didn't matter if it helped find Eliza's killer. Things were getting hot in Rebel Forge, and if it took some stirring to make things boil over, then I was going to do it.

"That was fast," Sara Lynn said as I returned her car keys to her.

"And yet I managed to annoy several people in that short a time," I said.

"Jennifer, are you being bad?"

I looked around. The only customers in her store were clustered back by the scrapbooking how-to books. "I'm trying to find out what really happened to Eliza. I have to believe that whoever killed her is the same person who took those shots at Bailey and me, and then burned down my old apartment."

"But why would they be so zealous?" she asked. "It doesn't make sense."

I didn't want to get into it right there with my sister. "Who knows why lunatics act the way they do?"

She studied me a few seconds, then said, "Jennifer, you've got a theory. What is it?"

"Me? I don't know what you're talking about."

"If you're trying to save me from some hurt feelings, I'm a little beyond that. I doubt you can tell me anything worse than I've already heard. Talk to me."

I took a deep breath, then said, "Okay, here's what I think happened. I think Bailey saw Eliza murdered, or at least witnessed something incriminating that the killer wanted silenced. The killer followed Bailey to Hurley's the night I was there with Greg, and he spotted your husband and me on the loading dock. I'm willing to bet he wasn't sure how long we were up there together, so he was afraid that Bailey told me whatever it was he was hiding."

"He didn't, did he? Don't worry, I won't tell Bradford if you're holding something back from him."

"I swear, he didn't tell me a thing," I said. "That's not completely true. He thought Eliza was seeing someone else, but that wasn't his secret. So anyway, the killer thinks I know, too, so I'm a target. That's why he burned Whispering Oak to the ground, to protect his secret."

"Then you think Bailey's dead, too," she said in a muted voice.

"I think no such thing," I said forcefully. "Bailey was fine the last time I saw him, and I don't have any reason to believe that anything has changed, and neither do you."

Sara Lynn stared off into space, then said, "I always thought it was sheer delusion when people said they knew when their loved ones died, but I don't anymore."

Chris answered the phone nearby, and said, "Jennifer, it's for you."

Sara Lynn fought to find a smile. "Now you're getting calls at my shop?"

"They probably want to ask me if I'm ever going back to mine," I said as I took the telephone.

"Jennifer Shane," I said.

"Jen, this is Savannah. You asked me about Eliza earlier, and I kind of cut you off. Since then I've been doing a little digging of my own."

"Savannah, how on earth did you know where to find me?"

"It was Lillian's idea to try there," she said, laughing. "Turns out that aunt of yours knows you pretty well."

I saw my brother's police cruiser pull up outside. The second I saw his face, I knew something bad had happened. "Savannah, can I call you back later? Something just came up."

"That would be fine," she said as she hung up. "But don't forget. I think this might be important."

As I placed the telephone back in its base, Bradford walked in and headed straight for Sara Lynn. He whispered something to her, and I saw her collapse. It was a good thing Bradford was ready for her fall. He caught her in his arms, and started back for the break room without missing a step.

"Bradford, what happened?"

"We identified the body at Whispering Oak," he said.

"It was Bailey, wasn't it?" Why had I blurted it out? Sara Lynn's prediction had spooked me, but that didn't mean I had to say it.

He frowned at me. "Now how in the world did you know that, Jennifer?"

"I didn't," I said as I pointed to our sister. "But she did. Sara Lynn just told me she knew that he died last night."

As Bradford laid her gently on the couch in back, he said, "You know I don't give any credence to that kind of thing."

"But she was right, wasn't she?"

He looked down at her. "It wasn't that hard a conclusion to jump to, given what's been going on around here lately." Bradford knelt down beside Sara Lynn and said, "Sis, can you hear me?"

Her eyelids fluttered, and she came fully awake. "What happened?"

"You fainted," I said over Bradford's shoulder. "But you're going to be fine."

"Then it's true? He really is dead?"

"I'm afraid he is," Bradford said. "We'd have known sooner, but there was a holdup with the dental records."

Sara Lynn started to get up, but Bradford put a hand on her shoulder. "Just keep still and collect your breath before you try to stand."

"Nonsense," she said. "I don't mind if you help me, but I won't let you hold me down. Do you understand me?"

He shrugged. "Whatever you say. Jennifer's going to take you home now. Where are your car keys?"

"I will not be handled," she lashed out at him, "no matter how good your intentions are. I'm not going anywhere. This is where I belong."

"You've lost it, woman. It's okay to show your emotions. Your husband just died."

"Don't you think I know that? I may never go back to that house. Every way I turn I'll see a memory of our lives together. What on earth makes you think I want that? I'm staying right here, Bradford, and you're going to have to arrest me to get me to leave."

I touched my brother's shoulder lightly. "I can stay here with her."

"You'll do no such thing," Sara Lynn said. "You have a store of your own to take care of. I'm warning you two right now, I won't be coddled. I've got Chris and Nancy. I'll be fine."

"Suit yourself," Bradford said. "I just thought you should know as soon as possible."

Sara Lynn sat up, and beckoned for him to join her. As he did, she kissed him on the cheek. "I know you do all you do for me out of love, but just being there for me is what I need right now. I'll call if I need you, okay?"

He looked at her steadily, then said, "Okay. Sara Lynn, I'm truly sorry for your loss."

"He wasn't the best husband in the world—not nearly as good a one as I'd thought, evidently—but I loved him more than I could imagine." She caught my glance, and though I didn't mean to voice my disapproval for the callous way she was handling her husband's death, something must have shown on my face.

"You don't approve of my behavior, do you, Jennifer?"

I jerked my gaze to the floor. "It's not up to me to approve or disapprove," I said.

"You're right, it's not," she said with the same bite she'd used on our brother earlier. "If I let myself accept what happened, I'm afraid of what I might do. I have to deal with this, in my own time and my own way. All I ask is that you support me through it."

"I would never dream of doing anything else," I said.

"That's fine, then. You both have jobs to do, so I suggest you get back to them."

Bradford and I started to walk out when Sara Lynn called, "Bradford, I have one question for you now."

"Anything," he said.

"Was it painful for him?"

I looked at my sister and saw a crack in her tough façade. I personally didn't know how she was managing as well as she was.

"No. One blow to the back of the head, with a shovel most likely. The coroner said it killed him instantly."

"Then there's that to take comfort in," Sara Lynn said.

"There is that," Bradford agreed, and the two of us walked out of the break room.

"I'm staying," I said once we were out of sight. "I don't care what she says."

"Jennifer, the worst thing in the world you can do right now is go against her wishes. You heard her. She'll call if she needs either one of us."

"We can't just leave her here," I said, tears coming to my eyes unbidden.

"We have to," he said as he walked me outside. "You don't remember Fluff, do you?"

"No, but I've heard you two talk about her enough

to feel like I knew her, too. She was your cat, wasn't she?"

He shook his head. "He was Sara Lynn's. He just tolerated the rest of us. Just before you were born, Fluff ran in front of a car. Poor thing didn't stand a chance. It nearly killed me, but Sara Lynn barely shed a tear. I thought she had a soul made of ice, until I found her outside two weeks later weeping silently over Fluff's grave. It took her a long time to come to grips with losing him, and until she did, she didn't shed a tear that I could see. Imagine how much worse this is going to be. The fact that Bailey was cheating on her in the end doesn't make it easier. It just makes it worse."

"How's that?" I asked.

"She wants to be mad at him, and who in the world could blame her, but she can't, because he's gone now and she'll never get the chance to make up with him. That's a lot to ask anybody to bear, wouldn't you say?"

"I guess you're right," I said. "I still wish there was something I could do."

"Until she asks for our help, you'll just do more harm than good if you try to interfere. Are you going back to the card shop? I'd be happy to give you a ride."

"No, thanks. I think I'll walk. I've got a lot on my mind."

"Okay, but if you need me, I'm just a phone call away."

After he was gone, I walked back to the card shop. Poor Bailey. I hoped the coroner was right. He'd been a fool to jeopardize his marriage with Sara Lynn for a fling with Eliza, but that didn't make him evil. He'd stuck by my sister in sickness and in health, and as far as I knew, he'd only strayed once. It didn't justify what he'd done, but he hadn't deserved to die for the mistake. I found myself wondering if Bradford suspected Sara Lynn at all in her husband's death. After all, he and his lover had both been murdered. What other conclusion could Bradford reach? Sara Lynn was one of the few people who knew Whispering Oak was going to be empty last night as well. I didn't care what Bradford thought, though. I couldn't imagine any circumstances that would turn my sister into a murderer.

So if my theory was right, which was a stretch—even I was willing to admit that—that meant the killer only had one loose end to tie up.

Me.

Chapter 13

"Did Savannah find you?" Lillian asked as I walked back into the card shop. "Jennifer, what's wrong?" My face must have given me away.

"Bailey's dead," I said, not meaning to just blurt it out. "It was his body they found in the house."

Lillian nodded. "Sara Lynn suspected as much, but I told her she was being paranoid." My aunt looked at me sharply. "Your sister must be devastated. So why are you here?"

"She didn't want me," I said, letting myself cry. Honestly, sometimes I could be such a girl.

"There, there, it's all right," Lillian said as she stroked my back. "It's nothing against you. Your sister always was one to stand strong. No doubt she threw Bradford out, too."

"She did," I admitted as I pulled away and dabbed at my tears. "I can't believe Bailey's dead."

"You can't? I've been slamming the man since I found out about his affair, and now I have all of that bad karma to live with." She patted my hand. "When your sister needs you, she'll let you know, and when that happens, drop everything and go to her. That's the best thing you can do for her."

"That's what Bradford said," I admitted. "But it's hard. I don't much feel like working today."

"Jennifer, aren't you worried about your own safety?"

I shrugged. "So you've come to the same conclusion I have. I'm the last target standing."

Lillian shivered. "What a wicked way to phrase it."

"It is a little too vivid, isn't it?" I admitted.

"So what do we do?"

"I'm more determined than ever to find out who killed Bailey and Eliza," I said. "I'll never believe the murders aren't related."

"Neither will I," she said. "Did you have any luck earlier?"

"Just in making half the town mad at me." I recounted what had happened with Addie, Kaye and Luke.

"My, you are leaving a wide band of hostility in your wake, aren't you? If one of them didn't want to see you come to harm before, they certainly do now."

"It's a gift, really," I said. I suddenly remembered putting Savannah off, so I grabbed the phone. "I need to make a quick call," I said.

"Be my guest. It's your shop," she said.

Savannah came on the line. "I'm so sorry about Bailey. I just heard. Could I speak with your sister?"

It was tough admitting that I'd bailed on her, but I really had no choice. Savannah was understanding, though. "Everybody deals with tragedy in their own way. When my grandfather died, my grandmother wouldn't cry for weeks. All she'd do was iron. When she ran out of clothes and sheets, that woman ironed towels, and even my daddy's socks. She'll come around. All she needs is time."

"I wanted to apologize for being so rude earlier. You had something to tell me."

"I'm not sure if it amounts to all that much, now

that I've had some time to think about it," Savannah said.

"Why don't you tell me, and I can judge for myself?"

"I suppose that's the best way to handle it, but I hate passing rumors along, especially when they might not be true."

"Savannah, I can't promise I won't tell Lillian, and Bradford if I have to, but I can say I won't breathe a word of it idly."

"I know you won't. Now I've made such a fuss about it you'll be sure to think I've lost my mind."

I waited, and a few seconds later, she said, "Okay, it's not much, but here goes. Pete and I were looking for our table at the banquet, and we saw someone take one of the letter openers from our table. At first I thought it was just some petty theft, but with what happened to Eliza, I'm beginning to wonder if it was more than that."

"Who was it?" I asked.

"A fellow who comes into the restaurant now and then. He's not a member of the chamber, so it kind of surprised me to see him there. Who knows? Maybe he walked in off the street and wanted a souvenir. Though with his kind of money, it would surprise me."

"Savannah, I've known you my entire life, and I've never known you to beat around the bush like this. Do you even know the man's name?"

"Of course I do," she said curtly. "There's another reason I don't want to say. It's because of that best friend of yours."

"Gail? What does she have to do with this?" And then I knew. "You saw Reggie Bloom take the letter opener, didn't you?"

"So you already know," she said.

"Not until a second ago. Thanks."

"Jennifer, be careful."

"You know it," I said as I hung up.

"Reggie Bloom?" Lillian asked. "What's he got to do with this?"

I held up a hand. "Give me a second." I started mulling over the possibilities that my new landlord's son could have been mixed up in the murder. I knew he'd looked familiar when I'd met him at dinner, but I hadn't been able to place him. Had I seen him at the banquet myself and not realized it? Gail had complained that she thought Reggie had been seeing another woman, and on the dock Bailey had told me that he thought Eliza was involved with someone else, too.

"Okay, I may be nuts, but listen to this." I told Lillian what I was thinking, and she followed my reasoning every step of the way.

"Call your brother," she said. "He needs to know about this."

"Do you honestly think we have enough to go to him?"

Lillian frowned. "Jennifer, Bradford can question him, can't he? What harm will that do?"

"What if I'm wrong?" I said. "Reggie's going to hate me."

"But what if you're right," Lillian replied. "You may be living on the grounds with a murderer. If anything happens to you, and we didn't tell Bradford, he'll kill me, so call your brother for my sake if not yours."

I picked up the telephone and dialed Bradford's number. When he answered, I said, "Do you have a minute to talk?"

"Sure, I was just about to take a break, and I'm in my office. Do you want to come over?" He was in

City Hall at the other end of Oakmont, a short stroll from my business.

"Okay, I'll be there in two minutes."

"Hang on a second. You know what? It's a pretty day. Why don't I walk over there? Do you have any coffee on?"

"You know it," I said.

"Then I'll see you in a minute or two."

After he hung up, I started having second thoughts. "Lillian, this is a mistake. I shouldn't have called him."

"So blame me for having the overactive imagination."

The door chimed, and I looked over to see who was coming in. Bradford must have sprinted to get there that fast. It was a customer, though, a welcome relief. She looked at a few cards, then asked, "Do you have anything edgier than these?"

"What did you have in mind?" I asked.

"I'm looking for something with some bite. My husband just told me he's leaving me for a younger woman, and I'd like to show him my disgust with a card. I figured, why not? They make cards for everything else."

Lillian smiled at the woman. "I've got just the card for you. In fact, I made it myself." As she led our customer to her selection of acerbic cards, Bradford walked in.

"Where's that coffee?" he said, then lowered his voice when he saw we had a customer.

"It's in back," I said as I led him to our storeroom that also served as a handy place for our breaks.

I poured him a cup, and one for me as well. He sipped it, then said, "That's great. Now what's up?"

"I'm not sure I should have called you," I admitted. "I'm starting to feel silly about it."

"What's it concerning?"

"Everything that's been happening in town the past few days," I said.

"Sis, if you have any ideas, I'll take them. This isn't for the general public, but I'm not doing too well. I know there's got to be a common link here, but I can't find it. If I don't come up with something soon, I'm going to have to call the state police, and I hate having to do that."

"Okay, but remember, this is just theory." I recounted Savannah's story about the letter opener, then told him my suspicions linking Reggie Bloom to Eliza.

"It's not much, is it?" he asked after he stared at his coffee for a few seconds.

"I'm sorry I called you," I said. "I guess I'm just grasping at straws."

"Sometimes that's the only way to find what you're looking for," Bradford said. "I'll have to be careful when I talk to him. His family's got money, and that means influence."

"Forget I said anything, Bradford."

He shook his head. "A lead's a lead, Sis. It won't cost a thing to question him." He took one last sip, then said, "Thanks for the coffee."

Before I could stop him, he was gone. Should I have kept my suspicions to myself? The way my imagination could run on overdrive, I'd be suspecting Pete next.

Lillian was ringing up a sale, and I could see that the woman had bought one of nearly every card my aunt offered. The woman was smiling as she looked at me. "These are wonderful. You should get them into every card shop in the country."

"Tell her that," I said, gesturing toward Lillian. "She's talented, isn't she?"

"With just the right twisted mind," the woman agreed.

Lillian shrugged. "It's a gift. Thanks for coming by."

"Thank you," she said, and then to everyone's surprise, she hugged Lillian before leaving.

"That was something," Lillian said, after the woman had gone.

"She's right, you know. Your cards would sell just about anywhere."

Lillian looked pleased, though she said, "You've been working with the glue too much lately; the vapors have gone to your head. What did your brother say?"

"He's going to talk to Reggie," I said.

"Wouldn't you love to be privy to that conversation?"

I straightened the bags under the counter as I said, "Not particularly. The man's not that fond of me now. Wait until Bradford talks to him."

"Jennifer, do you have any ideas about what we should do now?"

"We could always make some new cards. How's the inventory in your section?"

She said, "Let me check."

I walked over to Lillian's corner, and after she went through the racks, she said, "We've been selling more of these than I thought. I need to come up with some new cards."

"That's fine, but don't forget, you should replace the ones you're selling, too. After all, they're your most popular cards."

She looked hesitant, and I asked, "Is something wrong?"

"I have so much fun coming up with each card, but it's halved every time I have to do the same one again. It gets tedious, doesn't it?"

"It can," I admitted. "Mass production is a lot different from the initial creative process, but we can't sell them if they're not on the racks. Come on, I'll help you."

"With the themes?" she asked.

"Oh, no, we'll leave that up to you. What I can do is help you make replacements for the cards you've sold. I know it may seem a bit morbid working when the world's falling down all around us, but to be honest with you, I think it might just take my mind off what's been happening lately."

"Then by all means, let's make some cards."

I got out the stock and started folding cards while Lillian picked several of her cards that were running low. As I worked to replicate them, I couldn't help but laugh at some of the sentiments. After all, who could resist opening a card that said, "Dinosaurs, Pet Rocks and Drive-Ins" on the outside? Inside it, Lillian had written in a fine hand, "They're All Gone. Why Aren't You?"—a dry message expressed so cheerfully. We worked on several different cards, waiting on customers now and then. By closing time, we'd managed to restock most of her section.

"Any plans tonight, Jennifer?" Lillian asked.

"No, I'm going to stay home and hang out with Oggie and Nash. I've missed the rascals lately. How about you?"

"Another evening, another beau," she said, waving her hand in the air. "It can be difficult finding the right man in this town."

"Especially when you've already tried out so many of them," I said with a smile.

"My, don't you have a mouth on you."

"It's your fault," I said. "I've been reading your greeting cards all afternoon."

"Perhaps we should limit your exposure then," she said, adding a smile. "Have a nice evening, Jennifer."

"You, too," I said. Lillian left, but I still had a report to run on my register, and then there was the bank, inventory and supply restocking. It was definitely easier being an employee than an owner, but I didn't mind. Custom Card Creations was mine, and I wouldn't have had it any other way. After I was finished for the night, I decided to walk down to Sara Lynn's shop to see how she was doing, but I was surprised to see the place dark, though it was a night my sister normally stayed open late. Had she finally taken our advice and gone home? Despite what she'd said, I decided to go by and check on her. The only problem was, I still didn't have my car. Getting rides from my family was getting old. I wanted my independence back.

I phoned my brother. "I need a ride," I said abruptly.

"I'm fine, Jen, how are you?"

"Sorry," I said. "I'm just tired of depending on you for my transportation."

"Are you at the shop?"

"No," I said, "I'm in front of Forever Memories. Sara Lynn closed up early."

"I know, she called me," he said.

"Why didn't she tell me, too?"

"Take it easy, Jennifer. She tried calling you, but your phone was busy. She doesn't want to be disturbed, and I'm going to respect that wish."

"Fine, I'll leave her alone," I said, not at all happy about the way my sister was acting. "So, do I get that ride, or not?"

A horn honked nearby, and at first I was annoyed. Then I recognized the sound. I looked over at Bradford, who was behind the wheel of my Gremlin, holding his cell phone. The car's once-broken window was now bright and shiny.

"Hop in," he said.

"No way. You scoot over. I'm driving."

He did as I asked, though I could tell it was with reluctance. "Now I get to drive you around."

"Just to my office," he said. "I'm parked there. I thought you'd like your car back."

I rubbed the steering wheel. "You betcha."

"Hey, Sis, when are you going to get a car that was made in the last twenty years, anyway?"

I stroked the dashboard. "This car has character," I said.

"It's a character, all right," he replied with a grin.

"Don't talk that way about my baby. Did you speak with Reggie Bloom?"

"I did," Bradford admitted, and from the expression on his face, I could tell it hadn't gone well. "He wasn't pleased about our conversation."

"I'm sorry," I said. "I should have kept my mouth shut."

"Actually, you did the right thing. I was about to dismiss him when he started getting belligerent. That just makes me want to dig a little deeper. I didn't like his attitude."

"Bradford, don't make this personal. He had a right to be defensive."

My brother shook his head. "You don't understand. A lot of what I do is based on my gut. There was something that didn't jibe between the way he acted and what he was saying. It's not going to hurt anything to poke around a little."

"Just don't poke too hard," I said. "I'm living on his mother's goodwill, remember?"

"Speaking of your new place, have you had the locks changed yet? You don't know how many keys are floating around, and I'm willing to bet there are a couple at the main house."

"I'll speak to Helena," I said, "but I can't just

change the locks without her permission. Besides, I've got my guardians, remember?"

"If you're relying on Oggie and Nash as your home security system, you might as well leave your door wide open."

"Okay, as watch cats they're pretty useless, but other than that, they're adorable. I've still got my softball bat, and I know how to use it."

"Just watch your step, okay?"

"I promise," I said. I dropped him off at his office, made the bank deposit, and then drove to my new place. Funny, but the day before, I had felt secure living behind a locked gate. That serenity was gone now, knowing that a murderer might have the code himself. Could Reggie have done everything I suspected, or was he just a convenient suspect? If he was guilty, would my brother's questioning make him more cautious, or more reckless? He was a hard man to figure out.

As I got out of the Gremlin, I saw that someone was watching me from the trees.

"Hello?" I called out.

"Who's there?" I asked, wishing I had my bat with me.

Reggie himself stepped out, a cigarette in his lips. "I've been waiting for you," he said.

I jammed my keys between my fingers and made a fist in case I had to defend myself. "What do you want?"

"Did you sic your brother on me?"

He was angry; there was no doubt about that. "I don't know what you're talking about." Denial was my best course of action at the moment, at least until I got my bat.

Reggie grunted. "I think you do."

I started toward my door. "Think what you want."

As I slid the key into the lock, he said from behind me, "You need to mind your own business."

"You, too," I said for some inane reason, as I slipped inside and bolted the door. Bradford's point about the locks hit home, so I took a chair and jammed it under the knob. Nobody would be able to get in now, short of breaking the door down.

Oggie and Nash were sitting side by side staring at me when I looked up.

"You two think I'm crazy, don't you?"

Neither one of them denied it. "Well, I think you're both unbalanced, too. So how do you like that?"

I could have sworn they both looked at each other before they came to me. I sat down heavily on the couch, and they bumped me in greeting before curling up next to me. I stroked a cat with each hand, and immediately felt better. They were better than therapy as they purred in unison at my touch. After a while, I felt my blood pressure start to drop and my pulse slow. Maybe it was my imagination, but then again, maybe it wasn't.

Then there was a knock on the door, and all the good they'd done was wiped away. It appeared that Reggie was back for the next round.

Just in case, I grabbed the bat before I moved the chair and opened the door. Helena took it all in, then asked lightly, "Were you going to get a little exercise in?"

"Sometimes I take some swings to loosen up," I said, making it up on the spot. If she thought I was crazy, she was too polite to mention it.

"How athletic of you." She thrust a basket out at me, and I had to lay the bat down to take it. "This is for you."

"What's this?" I asked as I looked under a fancy napkin.

"I've been baking banana muffins, and I thought you might like some."

"That's so sweet of you," I said. How could that son come from her? "Won't you come in?"

"I don't want to disturb you," she said, and then the words died in her throat as she saw Oggie and Nash.

"You're most welcome to join me, but I should warn you, they take a long time to warm up to strangers."

She sat in my spot on the couch, and the scoundrels curled up with her as though they'd known her their entire lives. I felt a twinge of jealousy, but then realized they could probably sense another soul in need of their company. "What handsome fellows you two are," she said as she stroked them.

The rascals were eating it up. "That's extraordinary. I've never seen them act that way with a stranger before."

"We're not strangers," she said, talking to the cats more than she was to me. "We're just old friends who haven't met yet." After a few minutes, Helena looked up at me and said, "I understand you and Reggie had words tonight."

"Listen, I'm sorry if he's angry about Bradford questioning him, but my brother's the sheriff; that's his job."

"Dear, you don't have to explain it to me. I understand completely. Reggie really is a sweetheart. He's just been under a little pressure handling the family businesses. When his father got sick, Reggie had to step in and take over. I'm afraid it's made him cross and impatient at times, but give him a chance. You'll warm to him."

I couldn't imagine the circumstances where that would actually happen, but I knew enough to keep that opinion to myself. "Thanks for the advice," I said.

"But no thanks, am I right?" There was a smile on her face that showed her good nature. "Don't worry, I'll butt out." She stood, and the cats watched her carefully as she said to them, "It was an honor and a privilege spending time with you both. We must do it again sometime."

Oggie picked that moment to mew, and Helena looked delighted. "Why thank you, I had fun as well."

Helena looked at me and said, "You must think I'm dotty, having conversations with cats."

"We chat all the time," I admitted. "They're both great listeners, if you can get them to sit still long enough."

"Jennifer, thank you for sharing part of your evening with me."

"Thank you for your company, and the muffins."

She nodded, and paused at the door. "Oh, I almost forgot. A locksmith will be coming by tomorrow to replace your locks. I've instructed him that no one else is to have a key. Is that suitable?"

"Perfectly," I said.

She reached down and grabbed my bat, then handed it to me. "Until he arrives, I'd suggest you swing for the fences, isn't that what they say?"

I grinned as I took the bat from her. "It is. Good night, Helena."

"Good night to you all."

After she was gone, I cracked a window to let in some of the cool night breeze. I felt much better about my new living quarters after Helena's visit. Though Reggie was a definite concern, his mother was delightful. Perhaps she was right about her son. Could I have been wrong to judge him so quickly? After all,

I considered Gail to be a good judge of character, and she'd dated him for quite a while. How bad could he be? Then again, she'd begun to have second thoughts about him. Could he have killed two people? What could have driven him to murder? Then again, what makes anyone kill? I had other suspects—Addie, Kaye, Luke and Polly—and I wasn't ready to turn my back on any of them.

I was still wondering about which one of them might be a murderer when I heard a noise outside the cottage.

Someone was out there, and it was not my imagination.

Chapter 14

Without really thinking about it, I grabbed the bat and threw the door open.

"Come on out," I said. "Or I'm coming after you."

I didn't hear another sound for a few seconds, then I saw a squirrel scamper up a nearby tree. Could that have been the sound I'd heard from inside? I waited there in the growing darkness, but the only sound I heard was the squirrel scolding me from above.

"Jennifer, your paranoia is becoming amusing," I said as I went back inside. Still, I bolted the door and slid the chair back under the knob just as soon as I shut the window and locked it. I considered putting the bat back by the door, but I decided it would be better to have it close by. I fed the cats, then ate a few muffins and drank some milk. After that, I tried to watch a movie, but it couldn't hold my attention. An hour earlier than I was used to, I was ready for bed. Just in case, I threw the bat up onto the loft, and then climbed up myself. I knew I'd feel silly in the morning, but at the moment, it was all the comfort I needed to fall asleep, and that was what counted.

The next morning, I awoke to the sound of thunder and a heavy rain beating down on the cottage roof. It was still dark out, though the clock showed that the sun should have been up by now. I felt safe and snug in my new little nest, and I didn't want to leave it. Oggie and Nash got up and took turns stretching, something that always amazed me. It appeared that neither cat had a bone in their bodies as they arched their backs and spread their claws.

I delayed leaving as long as I could, but finally it was time to go to work. Though the Gremlin was parked less than fifteen feet away from my front door, I still got wet getting there, despite my umbrella.

It was a gray day, one that matched my mood as I opened the shop. Lillian came in a few minutes before we were scheduled to open, and I said, "I'm not sure you should have bothered. I doubt we'll get much foot traffic today."

To emphasize my point, a bolt of lightning lit up the gloom for a moment, followed quickly by a roll of thunder that shook the glass.

"Then we can make cards. Why don't you teach me something new?" she asked. "It's the perfect day for it."

"Do you really want to learn?" I said, my enthusiasm lagging for some reason.

"I've got it," Lillian said. "You can teach me how to quill. I've been wanting to learn for some time."

"It's not all that difficult," I said. "You just roll the strips up on the quilling tool, and then you glue them to your card."

"Show me," she said patiently.

I shrugged, then collected a few supplies. While I did that, Lillian cleared off our worktable by the window. She looked at the white strips I'd collected and said, "We can do better than that, can't we? Today calls for bold colors, wouldn't you say?" She was back in a second with a packet of long, thin strips in vibrant, energetic colors. "Now that should wake us up. Teach me."

I took a quilling needle, selected a bright orange strip, then rolled it tightly onto the tool. As Lillian tried to imitate me, I said, "Use your finger as a base, then roll the paper up, keeping tension on it all the time."

Once she had the tight circle, I took mine and said, "Now you can loosen the coil for whatever shape you'd like." I pinched one edge, let the other loosen a little, then pinched the other. "Make several of these and you've got a flower," I said. Lillian's result was not as crisp as mine was, but she was clearly delighted with the technique. "I've seen those hearts you make," she said. "Show me how to do them."

"They're really easy," I said, getting into the spirit of the lesson. I explained as I worked. "First you crease the paper along the short axis in the center of the strip. Then coil one side tightly all the way to the crease, and let it go. The paper will retain the shape. Do the other side, and you've got a perfect heart. All it needs is a little glue to secure it, and you're ready to add it to a card."

"It can't be as easy as you make it look," Lillian said.

"All you need are the right supplies and a little practice," I said. We made enough flowers and hearts to satisfy St. Valentine himself, having a great deal of fun as we worked.

By the time I looked out the window, I saw that the rain had stopped and the sun was actually trying to come out.

"That was fun," I told Lillian. "It's good having you here."

"It's good to be here," she said.

We were still basking in the warmth of our card-making session when the front door opened. I was surprised to see Kaye Jansen walk in.

"Good morning," she said before I could say a word. "Do you have any thank-you cards?"

"Of course," I said as I led her to them. "I'm surprised you don't have anything at the drugstore."

"I want something nicer than what we carry. George doesn't like to carry too much inventory he's afraid he won't be able to move."

"How do you like working for your father-in-law?" I asked.

"I'm not an employee, Jennifer," she snapped. "I own a piece of it, too. Now about those cards."

"We have a good selection over here," I said as I showed her some boxes. "If it's something special, I'd be delighted to help you make a personalized card yourself."

She rolled her eyes. "Thanks, but I don't think so. Your cards are cute and all, but not all of us have the time to fritter away making them." She grabbed a box of manufactured cards I carried and said, "These will do nicely. I'm giving them as thank you notes to everyone who donated something for the flowers. I'm sure you won't mind donating these to such a good cause," she said as she started to put them in her purse.

"I'll give them to you at cost," I said, "but I still have to pay for them myself. By the way, is that new?"

I pointed to a gold chain around her neck, adorned with a modest diamond pendant.

She said, "This? No, it's been in the family for years. I just don't wear it that often."

"Oh, my mistake. It looks expensive. So, will you be paying with cash or a credit card?"

Kaye looked at me for a second like she didn't believe me, and I knew she was waiting for me to back down. She could wait until I howled at the moon, she wasn't getting them for free.

Finally, reluctantly, she asked, "How much do you have to have?"

"Just give me half of the sticker price and we'll call it even."

"I think I'm in the wrong business," she said as she pushed a five on me.

At the door, she stopped and turned back. "Did you find Luke in time?"

"He changed his mind about leaving town," I said, though I didn't mention that I'd twisted his arm to secure his stay.

"How odd," Kaye said. "I thought we'd seen the last of him. Oh, if you're still looking for Polly, she came back this morning."

"That's earlier than you expected, isn't it?"

"She said something about it raining the entire time. I just thought you'd like to know."

Before she could leave, I had a sudden thought. "I heard you were talking to Bailey the night of the banquet."

"I don't know who told you that, but they're lying."

"Are you sure? He mentioned something to me before he died about seeing you. I must have been mistaken. Sorry."

"You should get your facts straight before you say anything," Kaye said, and then bolted out of the shop.

After she was gone, Lillian asked, "When did you find that out? I had no idea Bailey had talked to her."

"Maybe because it's not true," I admitted. "But Bailey saw someone that night, I'm sure of it. I wanted to test Kaye's reaction.

"She wasn't too pleased with it," Lillian said. "How much do you want to bet you won't be getting one of those cards?"

I waved the five in the air. "Her contribution was more than I'd hoped for."

Lillian laughed. "I thought she was going to have a stroke when you asked her to actually pay for them."

"Hey, I gave them to her at cost. Don't I get credit for that?"

"Of course you do. I don't blame you a bit. I hate when people try to strong-arm me into doing something."

I looked at her to see if she was kidding. My aunt was the queen of that particular technique, and pity the poor soul who caved into it even once, because from there on out, she'd own them.

I grabbed my jacket and asked, "Do you mind watching the shop? I'd like to talk to Polly."

"Do you still think she might have done it?"

"There's always a chance. Besides, it would be refreshing to be able to eliminate one of my suspects."

"Go, but don't stay too long. I thought we might go to The Lunch Box at noon."

"Lillian, you know how I hate to close the store."

She lowered her chin. "And yet you have no compunction about leaving me here alone to fend for myself."

"Fine, we can have lunch out. But I'm picking up the check."

"Not with that measly five, you won't."

I put the money in the register before I left. "I wouldn't dream of it."

"You should frame that instead of putting it into circulation," Lillian said. "You know how tight Kaye is with her money."

"Just for charity," I said. "She had a lot of nerve asking for donations when she was wearing that fancy necklace. Anyway, I'll be back by lunch."

"You'd better, or I'm going without you."

"You wouldn't do that," I said with a smile.

"And why not?"

"Because I'm buying, and you wouldn't miss that for the world."

"Of that I'm guilty."

I found Polly going through a book of real estate listings. The frown that was plastered to her face didn't break when she saw me standing at her desk.

"What do you want, Jennifer?"

"Gosh, I came by to look at houses, but now I'm not so sure I want to."

She studied me for a second, then forced a smile to her face. "Come on, don't hold that against me. I didn't mean to be curt with you. Of course I'd be delighted to show you some of my listings."

"You're back in town early, aren't you? I heard your trip was cut short because of rain."

"You've just got to love small towns," she said as she flipped through her book. "Now here's a property that would be just perfect for you."

Out of idle curiosity, I looked at the listing. "This has four bedrooms," I said. "That would leave an extra room even if I gave each cat their own space."

She glanced at the page, then said, "I'm sorry, that's the wrong one." The next one she flipped to had one bedroom, and barely had enough square footage to turn around in.

"What was this before," I asked, "a telephone booth?"

"No, the owner bought one of those garage kits and made it into a getaway. It's charming, isn't it?"

"All I can say from this is that it's tiny. Anyway, I've got a new place to live. I guess there's no rush."

"Where are you staying? That was a tragedy at Whispering Oak, wasn't it?"

I looked at her steadily. "How did you hear about that? I thought you were out of town."

Polly lowered her voice. "Please. I had breakfast at The Lunch Box. Do you honestly think anyone in town was talking about anything else? I'm so sorry for your loss. How's Sara Lynn taking it?"

"She's holding up," I said, uncomfortable with the way our conversation had shifted. At least Kaye had kept her empty condolences to herself. "Did you know Bailey very well?"

"Enough to speak to him in the grocery store or at a ball game, but nothing beyond that. Why do you ask?"

"I heard you knew him better than that," I said, stretching the truth beyond all recognition. "You spoke with him the night of the banquet, didn't you?"

"I saw a great many people that night," Polly said as she slammed the book shut. "Do you know what? I'm late for a showing. I nearly forgot all about it. Good-bye, Jennifer."

"We'll talk again later," I said.

"There's nothing left to discuss." Before she bolted away, she handed me a card. "If you change your mind about that garage, let me know."

"Oh, I will," I said. After she was gone, I threw her card away in her own trash can so she'd know exactly how I felt.

I wanted to tweak Reggie, Addie and Luke with the same statement, but my growling stomach insisted I take care of it first, so I headed back to the card shop to get Lillian.

When I walked in the door, one of my suspects was already there, and from the look on Reggie's face, he wasn't any happier to see me than I was to lay eyes on him.

"There you are," he snapped at me.

"Hi, Reggie. Did you come to buy a card?" My sweetness was purely artificial, and we both knew it.

"I came here to tell you to leave my mother alone."

"Is that an order? Because in case you didn't realize it, you don't get to tell me what to do." I saw Lillian smile at that, but I had to stay focused on Reggie.

"I'm warning you," he said gravely.

I never got to find out what he was warning me about, because Gail walked in the shop just then. She looked confused to see Reggie there, but it only took her a heartbeat to catch up. "There you are," she said. "I thought you were meeting me at the square."

"I am," Reggie snapped. "There was something I had to take care of first."

Gail looked at him, then shifted her gaze to me. "Has he been bothering you again?"

"We were just talking," I said. The last thing I wanted to do was come between Gail and her boyfriend.

"Jennifer Shane, I asked you a question. Don't make me repeat myself. What did he say?"

I kept silent, so Lillian piped up happily, "He just threatened her, actually. He demanded that Jennifer stay away from his mother, and when she refused, he was getting ready to push her, but you walked in first."

Gail looked at me for confirmation, and I nodded unhappily.

Then she turned to Reggie. "That's it; we're through."

"What are you talking about?"

"You can't threaten my best friend and expect me to forget about it. I won't date a man who doesn't respect women."

He wanted to say something, I could see it in his eyes, but finally he threw up his hands and said, "Forget it. You're not worth this kind of trouble, anyway."

After he was gone, I saw Gail sag a little. I put my arm around her and said, "He wasn't worth it."

"I know," she said, "but I had hopes."

"We all do, dear," Lillian said. "Now why don't I treat you ladies to lunch?"

"It's my turn to pay," I protested.

Gail said, "I should be the one picking up the check. I knew he was wrong for me, but I needed you two with me to break up with him. That should earn you each a free lunch, at the very least."

"Why don't we all go dutch?" I asked. "That way everyone gets to buy."

They both laughed, and the solemn mood was broken. It wasn't until we got to The Lunch Box that I realized I hadn't had a chance to confront Reggie about being with Bailey at the banquet. It would have to wait until another time, but not until he cooled down first. I didn't have that much time.

We found three stools together near the window in the serpentine ribbon of seats. The Lunch Box was hopping, with Savannah ruling over the counters, and Pete grilling in back. Savannah came over as soon as we sat down. "Hello, ladies. Oh, and hi, Lillian." The two of them had been friends forever, and they'd cut their pleasantries to acerbic jabs, though I knew they were as close as sisters.

We were all surprised when Lillian replied, "You're looking fit today. Have you lost weight?"

Savannah's eyes narrowed. "Maybe a pound or two. Why?"

"Why not? How'd you like to lose another one?"

"Go on," Savannah said. "I'm listening."

"If you'll round up three glasses of tea, I'll tell you."

Savannah returned in no time and put the glasses

in front of us. Lillian took a sip, then leaned forward. "Okay, here goes. Exercise more, and eat less."

Savannah whooped with laughter, though I thought the humor was a little lacking. "I was getting worried about you, but I can see you're just as mean as ever."

"Does a snake jog in tennis shoes?" Lillian asked her.

"He does if he's running a marathon," Savannah said as she walked away.

Gail looked at me and raised her eyebrows in question. "Don't worry, I don't get much the two of them say, either. They've known each other so long they have their own code."

She shrugged. "Like the time we went to that movie?"

"Popcorn's cheaper than glue," we both said in unison. A man in front of us kept repeating that phrase until an usher had to physically remove him from the theatre, and Gail and I had adopted his catchphrase as our own.

Lillian asked, "What are you two nattering away about?"

"I guess you had to be there," I said. Maybe Gail and I were developing a code of our own. "Excuse me, I'll be right back." I'd been facing the door, and I could swear I'd seen Addie walk in the restaurant before turning away. "Hey, wait a second," I said as I rushed out after her. She ducked into a car parked at the side of the restaurant, and I was shocked when I realized that Luke was driving. I tapped on the window before they could escape, and she reluctantly rolled the window down.

"What do you want?"

"I didn't know you two were dating," I said.

"Don't be ridiculous. But even if we were, it wouldn't be any of your business," Addie said.

I looked over at Luke. "Boy, when you decide to stay, you really move back in, don't you? How long has this been going on?"

He got out of the car, and I suddenly realized how stupid I'd been confronting him like that without anyone backing me up. As I edged back to the entrance, he said, "I want to talk to you."

"I don't have anything to say to you," I said.

"That didn't stop you at the gas station, did it?"

I looked around for help, but I was all alone. "Trying to leave made you look guilty," I said. If I was going to get bashed, I might as well deserve it.

Instead of pressing me, he said, "I would never hurt Eliza. And neither would Addie."

"How long have you two been going out?"

"We aren't dating," he snapped, then looked back at Addie.

"So what are you two doing out together?"

He kicked at the dirt, then said, "We're doing the same thing you are. We're trying to figure out who killed Eliza. Is that so hard for you to believe? You're not going to like our number-one suspect. It's your sister."

"You've lost your mind," I said. Why did it surprise me that someone else was trying to solve the case besides Lillian and me? It wasn't like we had some right to meddle in other people's lives. But I didn't have to like the fact that Luke and Addie suspected my sister. "So what's your proof?"

"You're kidding, right? If she weren't your sister, you'd be all over her right now. Her husband was cheating on her with Eliza, and then he turns up dead, too? If Sara Lynn wasn't the sheriff's sister, she'd be in jail right now. The whole town thinks so."

"Maybe my brother knows something you don't," I said.

"What's that?"

"The fact that Sara Lynn is innocent."

Luke shook his head. "They all say that, don't they?" He took another step toward me, and hissed, "It's time you got what you deserved."

I was ready to run for the front of the restaurant when the back door opened and Pete came out with a bucket of hot grease. I'd never been so happy to see the man in my life.

"Jennifer, your friends were wondering where you got to," he said as he stared at Luke.

"I was just chatting, but I'm finished now." I didn't even wait to see what Luke's reaction was. Addie had waited in the car, but she'd been watching us the entire time, no doubt taking in every word.

"Then I suspect you should get back to them," Pete said.

Without a word, Luke got into the car and drove off.

"Thanks," I said. "I'd kiss you, but Savannah would swat me with a rolling pin."

"Might just be worth it for both of us," Pete said with a wicked grin on his face.

To his surprise, I leaned forward and kissed his cheek. "That was perfect timing," I said.

His face reddened slightly. "Go on, get back in there." I couldn't tell if he was pleased by my kiss, or just embarrassed. Maybe it was a combination of both.

I went back inside and took my seat.

"You were gone, so we ordered for you," Gail said.

"You're getting barbeque," Lillian added.

"Great. Here I was having trouble deciding, and you two step in and save the day."

Lillian looked at me for a few seconds. "Where were you?"

"I ran into Luke and Addie out in the parking lot. It turns out they're looking into the murders, too."

Lillian snorted. "What do they expect to find that we won't? Amateurs."

"That's what we are," I said as I took a sip of tea.

"Jennifer, we've helped the police from time to time in the past. I think that gives us standing, don't you?"

I didn't know how to answer that, and looked over at Gail, who was grinning as she hung on every word. "What are you smiling about?"

"You two are more entertaining than daytime television."

I was saved from replying by our food order arriving. Savannah slid plates in front of Lillian and Gail, but left before giving me anything. "Hey, where's mine?"

Savannah turned around. "Did you say something?"

"I was just wondering where my food was," I said.

She got close enough for me to smell her perfume. "Did you kiss my man?"

Was she serious? I'd just been thanking a guy I'd known my entire life. "Yes, ma'am, I admit it. He did me a favor, and I thanked him politely."

"Where did you kiss him?" she asked.

"By the side of the restaurant," I answered.

It was touch and go for a second, then Savannah whooped with laughter. "Lillian, she's more like you than you're willing to admit."

"You take that back," I said, smiling.

"I won't do it," Savannah said as she retrieved my plate from Pete's window.

I stuck my tongue out at him. "Tattletale."

He ducked back, as if he was worried I'd hurl one of the tiny hush puppies at him. They were light, crisp and golden, and I wouldn't have willingly given one up for the president.

As we ate, Lillian asked, "So what do you make of our crime-busting competition? Did they say who they suspect?"

I mumbled, hoping she would let it slide, but I should have known better. "Jennifer, I can't understand you with a mouthful of food."

"Really?" I said as I put another forkful of barbequed pork in my mouth.

Gail said, "She doesn't want to say in here."

"Really? I had no clue that was what she was doing." Lillian leaned toward me and added, "They suspect Sara Lynn, don't they?"

I nodded. "You really can't blame them."

"Of course I can," Lillian said, ignoring her salad completely. "Jennifer, it's time we put an end to this."

"I'm trying," I said. "If you have any more ideas, I'm willing to hear them out."

Gail looked at us both, then asked, "Do you two really think you can solve a case that Bradford can't? I hate to say it, but that's kind of arrogant of you, isn't it?"

"You have no idea," I admitted. "The thing is, he's got rules he has to follow, and we just keep poking our noses into other people's lives until we find out what we're looking for."

"Isn't that dangerous?"

"It can be," I said, "but that's just a part of it. What matters is that the truth comes out, one way or another."

Gail shook her head. "I don't know how you do it."

"The same way we do everything else," Lillian said. "With panache and great flair. Now, if you two are finished, we all have work to do."

Back at the card shop, Gail said, "Thanks for everything."

"We didn't do anything," I said.

"You did more than you could know. I just hope I didn't make your life harder than it has to be, breaking up with Reggie like that."

"Believe me, I'll be fine."

After she was gone, Lillian said, "Now what do we do to stir things up? I'm ready for some action."

"I've been poking and prodding like mad, but I don't seem to get anywhere."

"Then it's time we stepped things up," Lillian said.

"Do you have any idea how we can do that, short of an outright accusation?"

"Give me a minute," she said.

"You can have all afternoon," I said. "I'm not going anywhere."

"Don't be so sure about that," Lillian said. "I think I've got an idea how to flush the killer out."

"It sounds like it's going to be dangerous," I said.

"Are you afraid?"

"A little," I admitted.

"Good. If you weren't, I'd be worried about you. We'll make this as safe as we can. Now here's what we're going to do. You've been pussyfooting around with hinted accusations, but I want to come right out and accuse everyone."

"What? You can't be serious," I said. "We can't do that without any justification. They'll all laugh in our faces, and we'll deserve it."

"Do you have a better idea?"

"Doing nothing is better than making fools of ourselves. We need to approach the situation with less randomness, you know?" I went for the whiteboard. When Lillian saw what I was doing, she said, "Jennifer, this is a time for action, not deliberation."

"Lillian, I love you, you know that, but this time,

you're wrong." I propped the board up and studied it. "There's got to be a key here somewhere, if we're just smart enough to see it."

She frowned at the board. "Do you honestly think so?"

"I do," I said.

"Then where is it?" We'd filled the board with scribbled motives, since everyone on our list had the means and the opportunity, including Reggie.

"Why does anyone kill?" I asked.

"We've been over this a dozen times, Jennifer. Let's focus on the basics."

I erased the board, despite my aunt's protests. "What are you doing?"

"Are you trying to tell me you haven't memorized that board, too? I'm willing to wager either one of us could recreate it if we had to."

"Fine, do it your way." She was testy, but I knew Lillian was frustrated with the murders and not with me.

The fresh board mocked me. "Why aren't you writing?" Lillian asked me.

"There's something I'm missing, something I heard over the past few days that I'm not getting. It's the key, I just know it."

"Well, think, Jennifer! What is it?"

"That's not helping," I said.

"Maybe if you take a walk, it will come to you," Lillian said. "I don't mind watching the card shop."

It was true that there were two things that always got my juices flowing: either a walk or a shower. Since I didn't have a shower handy, a walk made perfect sense. "You're right, I need to jar loose whatever is lodged in my head. I don't know how long I'll be," I said as I headed for the door.

"You're not on a schedule," she said. "You own this place, remember?"

I was nearly outside when Lillian added, "One thing before you go. If it does come to you, don't do anything without me, Jennifer."

"I'm not crazy," I said.

"That's a discussion for another day," Lillian said. "But you can't deny you're rash at times."

"I like to think of it as active," I said.

"Call it what you will. I just don't want you taking any chances."

"Fine, I'll behave myself," I promised as I left the card shop. Since I had no destination in mind, I decided to start up Oakmont toward Sara Lynn's shop. At Greg's Pottery, I paused to look inside. He was having an earnest conversation with Stephanie, and I could swear it looked like he was proposing! Though he wasn't down on one knee, there was something the size of a ring box in his hand, and she kept looking at it as he spoke. I knew Greg had a tendency to ask women to marry him—after all, he'd asked me twice himself—but it was all I could do not to bust through the door and tell him he wasn't ready for such a big step. My hand was on the doorknob before I jerked it away. If Greg wanted to marry Stephanie, there was nothing I could do about it, and more important, there was nothing I should do to stop him. He had his life to live, and I had mine. If he believed Stephanie was what it would take to make him happy, then more power to him. Now if I could only convince myself of that.

I left the storefront and tried to put what I'd just seen out of my thoughts. I had something more important to deal with. As I walked, I thought about everyone involved with the murders. Eliza had plenty of enemies, but poor Bailey hadn't had any, as far as I'd known. Addie and Luke had been off base with their belief that Sara Lynn was the murderer. I knew my sister didn't do it, and no amount of proof would convince me otherwise. So how about the two of them? Addie inherited a business and was probably going after Eliza's ex-husband. She was basically taking over her partner's life before she was even in the ground. That smacked of motive. Then there was Luke. He'd professed his love for his ex-wife often enough. Would her scorn be enough to drive him to murder? Polly and Kaye had their own reasons to dislike Eliza, but again, did they hate her enough to murder her?

And there was Reggie. He was the dark horse in all of this. I didn't even have any proof that he'd been having an affair with Eliza. And even if he had been, why would he kill her? The most he had to lose was his relationship with Gail, and it was pretty obvious it hadn't been that important to him—not by the way he blew her off earlier. That left me with a ragtag collection of suspects, with conflicting motives to want Eliza dead.

I was at the park bench at the square, and I decided to stop walking to see if I could sort this mess out. I knew motive was the key, but what if I had the wrong one for one of my suspects? Eliza also ran an accounting business on the side—nothing too big, but she did taxes for several of the shop owners in town. Could her murder have been committed to cover up something else—a crime that had nothing to do with jealousy or anger?

Then I remembered what had been nagging at me all along, and it all fell into place. I started toward the business where I knew the murderer was working, forgetting all about my promise to Lillian to come get her when I figured it out.

Chapter 15

Wouldn't you know it? The business was deserted when I walked in. Why couldn't this have happened in the full swing of tourist season, when there was no place in town that wasn't crawling with visitors? I took a deep breath at the door, then moved toward the counter.

She looked up at me as I approached. "Jennifer. Don't you ever stay at your shop any more? I don't know how you do it."

"My aunt's watching the place." I looked around. "Where is everyone?"

"Thad's on break," Kaye said. "He won't be back for a while. Was there something I could help you with?"

I took a deep breath, then said, "You could save us all a lot of trouble and confess," I said, the words sounding insane even as I spoke them.

"Confess to what?" She held steady, but I could see her face blanch slightly at my prompt.

"You killed Eliza, and then you got rid of Bailey and tried to do the same thing to me when you thought we both knew what you'd done. You want to know the funny thing? I didn't put it all together until just a minute ago."

"I don't know what you're talking about," she said. "You're not well."

"You're the one who's sick," I said. "You're a murderer, Kaye."

"Why on earth would I kill Eliza?" she demanded. "We weren't friends, but I had no reason to hate her."

"I'm guessing that you did," I said. "Between her two businesses, Eliza had more money at her disposal than you could dream of. You never could stand the fact that Thad relied on his dad's income to keep you two solvent, could you? Everybody in town knows that you married him for money he didn't have. That's not the only reason you killed Eliza, though I'm certain it was a contributing factor in the end."

She looked more angry than flustered, but I knew I was right. "So what? Even if she did flaunt her money in my face, that didn't mean I wanted her dead."

There was just one thing for me to do. I had to press her harder until I got her to confess. "Like I said, it wasn't the only reason you killed her, but I've got a strong idea what your original motive was. Eliza found out you were stealing from the business when she started doing the books, didn't she?"

That hit home. She jerked her head back as if I'd smacked her. "You're just guessing, Jennifer."

"Kaye, the last time I was here, you didn't ring up a big sale as you made it. You told the customer the register was broken, but it was working fine, wasn't it? I watched you do it, and it never occurred to me what you were up to until later."

She shook her head back and forth vigorously. "I remember that. The register really was broken that day," she said, but the conviction in her voice was gone.

"It's a good way to steal, isn't it? But you had to know that you'd get caught as soon as your husband or father-in-law took an inventory. You decided to worry about that later, though, didn't you? I'm guessing you were trying to make up for the money you stole outright from the business before anybody else found out what you were up to. How did you get Eliza to keep quiet? I'm just curious, though it's really not that important. My brother will be able to figure it all out once he gets the state police and their team of forensic auditors in here."

I started for the door, and Kaye asked, "Where do you think you're going?"

"I'm getting Bradford," I said. "Don't leave until he gets here."

She laughed in such an odd way that it made me look closely at her. I don't know why I was so surprised, but Kaye had a gun pointed at me.

I couldn't believe the woman's audacity. She really was out of her mind. "What I don't understand is why you had to kill Bailey? Did he see something he shouldn't have?"

Kaye shook her head. "He denied it, but I know he saw me stab that witch. I couldn't let him turn me in, could I?"

"I don't understand why he didn't just call Bradford if he knew something."

Kaye gave me a smile, but it was devoid of warmth or pleasure. "I told him I'd kill Sara Lynn if he whispered a word about what he'd seen, and then the fool went and told you on the loading dock. I can't believe I missed. I had you both in my sights."

"He never told me anything that night," I said.

"Why should I believe you?"

I stared at her, and said, "Why should I lie?"

"My mistake, then," she said as she appeared to take it in. "You know it all now, though. Sorry, but that means that you've got to die."

"Kaye, do you honestly think you can get away with killing me now?"

She narrowed her eyes, then said, "Jennifer, you came in here today to rob me, and I had to defend myself. Your business can't be doing that well. I'm willing to bet I can get the state police to believe it, and after I have them on my side, your brother won't have any choice but to go along with their conclusions."

There was a wild look in her eyes that shook me to the core. I had to find a way through her fog so she'd know how delusional she was. "There is no way on earth that anyone is going to buy that, especially my brother." I had to wonder if the woman truly was insane.

She appeared to consider it for a few seconds, then asked, "Okay, if that's no good, how about this? You came in to chat and I was cleaning my revolver on the counter. You wanted to see it, and it accidentally went off as I handed it to you. Those things happen all the time. I'll be able to sell that story to your brother, once I have it staged."

And knowing her, she just might be able to pull it off. I only had one chance, and I had to take it quickly before she squeezed that trigger. I knocked over a display with my foot, and as her crazed glare shifted toward it, I picked up a large bottle of perfume on the counter and threw it at her. As Kaye ducked, I dove behind one of the aisles as a bullet shattered a vase near my head.

"There goes your accident theory," I shouted. "You might as well give up now. You're not getting away with it."

The gun barked again, and a lamp exploded into a thousand pieces, stinging my face and my right arm with shrapnel.

"I don't care what it looks like now," she screamed. "I just want you dead."

From the back of the store, we both heard a voice say, "Drop it, Kaye."

It was Thad. I looked back to see Kaye's husband with a gun of his own trained on her. Instead of doing as she was told, she shifted her aim and shot at him instead. Thad staggered back, but not before he got off a shot of his own. My ears were ringing from the gunfire in the small store as I saw Kaye fall back against the counter. The smell of spent gunpowder was heavy in the air, and there was a haze that stung my eyes.

The thing that struck me the most was that Kaye had the oddest expression on her face as she was hit, as if she couldn't believe her browbeaten husband had actually had the nerve to shoot back.

He'd done a good job of it, too. I glanced at Kaye's motionless form. There was nothing I could do for her. I dialed 911, and told Bradford's dispatcher that there had been a shooting, and that they needed to send an ambulance to the drugstore. The daft woman on the line was still asking me questions as I threw the telephone down and raced back to Thad. He'd been hit in the shoulder, and his face was milky white.

"How is she? Did I hit her?"

"Don't worry about that right now," I said. "You're bleeding."

"There's gauze over there," he said as he gestured to the first-aid aisle. I grabbed a roll, ripped off the wrapping, and handed it to him. As Thad pressed it to his shoulder, he said, "What do you know. Having a drugstore finally came in handy."

He tried to get up, but I wouldn't let him. "Jennifer, I need to make sure she's all right."

"She's not going anywhere," I said. "And you shouldn't move."

He must have seen something in my eyes, because he started to cry. "I love her. I know I shouldn't, but I do. I wasn't stupid enough to believe that she wanted me for anything besides money. I never should have tricked her into thinking I had any, but I wanted to marry her more than anything else in the world. I didn't have any choice, Jennifer. I had to shoot her. She was going to kill you."

"You did the right thing," I said as I stroked his hand. By the time Bradford got there, we were both crying. I wasn't sure why I was so openly weeping. Probably an aftereffect of being shot at.

Bradford asked softly, "Jennifer, are you hurt?"

"No, I'm fine," I said.

"You've got blood on your arm," he said.

I looked down and saw that one of the pieces of lamp must have cut me. "It's nothing. Is the ambulance on its way?"

"It's right behind me," he said. "What happened?"

"Let's get him taken care of, then I'll tell you."

"I wish I could do it that way, I honestly do," my brother said. "But I need to know right now."

Thad said, "It's all right. I'll tell him. My wife killed Eliza and Bailey. She was trying to kill Jennifer, too, so I had to shoot her." Then he started sobbing again.

"Is that the truth?" Bradford asked.

"Every bit of it," I said. "He saved my life."

My brother squeezed Thad's hand. "Thank you."

All Thad could manage was a nod, his eyes still staring ahead. It was almost as if he could see his wife's body, though she wasn't visible from where we were. The paramedics came, and soon had him on his way, strapped onto the same gurney I'd ridden on before.

One of them looked at me, and asked, "Are you all right?"

"It's just a scratch," I said.

"Don't worry," Bradford said. "I'll take her to the hospital myself."

"It's not that bad," I said, though I doubted anyone heard me.

There was a scream as they took Thad past Kaye's body, and then there was nothing but silence.

Finally, Bradford said, "Let's get you to the hospital. On the way, you can tell me why this all happened."

"What about Kaye?"

Bradford shook his head. "I don't doubt the shot killed her instantly. Jody and Hank are out front. Nobody's going to disturb the scene while I'm gone."

I grabbed another roll of gauze and dabbed at my arm. "It's barely a scratch. You need to be here. I can take myself to the hospital."

"I don't think so," he said, obviously reluctant to leave the crime scene. Bradford called out to Jody and Hank. "I need one of you to take my sister to the hospital."

I was surprised when Hank said, "I'll do it."

"I want Jody," I said in a whisper.

"Tough, I need him here. Don't worry; Hank's a good guy once you get to know him."

"Fine," I said. My arm was starting to sting a little, and I wondered if the shock was just starting to wear off, or if it was finally setting in.

"I'll be there soon," Bradford said. "Don't go anywhere."

"Where would I go?"

I averted my eyes as I walked past Kaye's body. It

was only partly because I felt squeamish, but mostly it was because I didn't ever again want to look at the woman who had widowed my sister. She was a killer twice over, and as far as I was concerned, she'd gotten exactly what she'd deserved.

I needed four stitches for the cut on my arm. At least my wrist was feeling better. Bradford walked into the exam room just as they were finishing up with me. To my surprise, Lillian was right behind him.

She hugged me, then said, "What did I tell you about going off on your own?"

"I forgot all about it," I admitted. "Sorry."

Bradford said, "I hate to break this up, but I need to interview my witness."

"Go right ahead," I said. "I'm ready to talk about it now."

Bradford turned and looked at Lillian, but before my brother could say a word, she said, "If you think I'm leaving, you're insane."

"This is official police business," Bradford said.

I interrupted him. "Could she stay here if she promises to keep quiet? I don't want to have to tell this more than once."

"Then wait for me," Sara Lynn said as she walked in. "I need to hear this, too."

Bradford clouded up for a second, but he finally said, "I give up. You two can listen, but not a word out of either one of you. I expect your promises."

After they both pledged their solemn oaths, Bradford looked at me, and said, "Go ahead."

"Do you want to hear what happened, or how I figured it out?" I asked.

"Why don't you start with your reasoning, and I'll interrupt if I have to. And Jennifer, make it as succinct as you can."

I looked at him and said, "Kaye Jansen killed Eliza and Bailey, then tried to kill me. Thad shot her before she could do that, though."

He shook his head. "I know that much."

"You said to be brief," I reminded him.

"Okay, then," he said as he ran a hand through his hair. "Let's hear the long version."

"Kaye was cheating her father-in-law by falsifying the books and failing to ring up sales. Eliza must have caught her doing it while she was working on her fraud, and gave Kaye time to make restitution. She started stealing from the store to make up the money, and Eliza probably called her on it. Kaye killed Eliza, and for some reason she thought Bailey witnessed it. Maybe she saw him leaving, or just thought she did. I don't suppose we'll ever know. Anyway, for whatever reason, Kaye tracked Bailey down, found him at Whispering Oak, then she killed him." I glanced over at Sara Lynn, but she looked like she was taking the news as well as could be expected. "Kaye thought I was upstairs, so she started the fire to take care of both of us. When I confronted Kaye about the theft, she tried to kill me, then Thad stepped in."

"But how did you know she'd been stealing?" Lillian asked, then immediately clapped a hand over her mouth.

Bradford didn't say a word, so I answered. "She was wearing a diamond necklace when she came to ask me for money, and Kaye was always complaining about how little money she had. Then when I went by to talk to her one day, I noticed that she failed to ring up a sale, and a pretty large one, at that."

"That wasn't much to go on," Bradford said.

"I know it wouldn't be enough to bring to you, but it was good enough for me. I honestly never thought Kaye would try to shoot me."

"No, why would you think that?" Bradford asked. "After all, she'd just managed to kill two other people to hide her secret. What on earth made you think she'd stop with two?"

"I just didn't think, I guess," I said.

Sara Lynn stepped up and hugged me. "Thank you, Jennifer."

"I didn't really do anything," I said.

"You found my husband's killer," she said. "Now if you'll excuse me, I have a funeral to plan." And then Sara Lynn broke down. I'd never heard her cry so fiercely. A doctor poked his head through the curtain as Bradford wrapped her up in his arms. He waved the doctor away as Lillian and I joined them in a familial embrace. It was time to mourn, now that Sara Lynn knew the truth, and we'd do the best we could to help her through it. After all, when it came down to it, that was what family really was all about.

CARD-MAKING TIPS

One of the techniques mentioned in this book is quilling. It's amazing what you can do with a quilling needle, some paper and your imagination. By wrapping thin strips of paper tightly and then manipulating them, you can easily make circles, ovals and many other shapes. Besides creating the three-dimensional flowers and hearts that Jennifer and Lillian make in this book, you can fabricate wreaths, balloons, clouds or even automobile tires! You can cut your own strips, but it gets tedious, and besides, most craft stores sell precut, multicolored strips ready to work with.

Have fun, and don't be afraid to experiment. That's one of the real advantages of card making. Most of the supplies are inexpensive enough to play with, and some of my favorite techniques and designs have come about because I achieved different results from what I was originally trying to create.

About the Author

Elizabeth Bright is the pseudonym for a nationally best-selling mystery author. Though never credited with solving a murder in real life, Elizabeth's alter ego has created scores of handcrafted greeting cards over the years.

Deadly Greetings

A Card-Making Mystery

by Elizabeth Bright

Getting customers into Custom Card Creations is hard enough. Now Jennifer is getting plenty of unwanted visitors—like a ghost in her new apartment, a pushy downstairs neighbor, her ex-fiance, and a drunken deputy. Then one of her most beloved card club members, Maggie, is killed in an accident—or was it? When Jennifer receives a card written by the victim before she died, referring to someone trying to murder her, she must investigate before she loses another good customer to more grim tidings.

"Elizabeth Bright shines in this crafty new series."
—**Nancy Martin, author of the**
Blackbird Sisters **mysteries**

0-451-21877-9

Available wherever books are sold or at penguin.com